PUFFIN BOOKS

Wyvern Summer

Toby Forward was born in Coventry. He went to college to pursue theological training and subsequently became a parish priest. He is now a full-time writer, and lives with his wife and two daughters near Hull.

Michael Foreman is one of the leading children's illustrators working today, and has won numerous prestigious awards. He spends his time with his wife and sons partly in London and partly at his house in St Ives, Cornwall.

For Catherine

PUFFIN BOOKS

Published by the Penguin Group
Penguin Books Ltd, 27 Wrights Lane, London W8 5TZ, England
Penguin Books USA Inc., 375 Hudson Street, New York, New York 10014, USA
Penguin Books Australia Ltd, Ringwood, Victoria, Australia
Penguin Books Canada Ltd, 10 Alcorn Avenue, Toronto, Ontario, Canada M4V 3B2
Penguin Books (NZ) Ltd, 182–190 Wairau Road, Auckland 10, New Zealand

Penguin Books Ltd, Registered Offices: Harmondsworth, Middlesex, England

First published by Andersen Press Limited 1994
Published in Puffin Books 1995
1 3 5 7 9 10 8 6 4 2

Text copyright © Toby Forward, 1994
Illustrations copyright © Michael Foreman, 1994
All rights reserved

The moral right of the author and illustrator has been asserted

Printed in England by Clays Ltd, St Ives plc

Wyvern Summer

Toby Forward

Illustrations by
Michael Foreman

I would contrive and paint
Woods, valleys, rocks and plains, dells, sounds and wastes,
Lakes which, when morn breaks on their quivering bed,
Blaze like a wyvern flying round the sun.

Browning

PUFFIN BOOKS

ONE

'Look!' she shouted. 'It's a dragon! See! A beauty!'

The man caught up with the girl. He was not old, but he still preferred not to run in that heat.

'Yes. Who'd have thought it?' He stared down at the flat, round stone, with the carved dragon, wings outstretched, mouth wide.

'This is a dragon's home,' said the girl.

'Well, now. I guess you may be right at that.' His voice was slow and deep.

They stood and looked around. For as far as the eye could see, fields and hills, and a clear sky. Just over one hill the point of a spire pointed high, topped by a weather vane. But close to, surrounding them, was a ring of tall, rugged grey stones, making a circle. The flat stone with the dragon-carving was set in the earth, in the centre of the ring. From side to side the circle was about as far across as a circus tent.

'Some of these stones are missing,' said the girl. She turned round, pointing to each in turn with a slim finger. Most of the stones were about the same distance apart, but there were some gaps. 'Are they doorways?'

'I'm glad you asked me that, Franny,' he said, 'because that's about the only thing I know about the whole business.'

'And?'

'And they're not gates, or doors. They were all there, once, all the same distance apart, give or take.'

'So what happened?'

'The Stonekiller smashed them.'

'You're kidding?'

'No.' He grinned down at her.

'Why?'

'You don't like archaeology,' he teased her. 'It's a lot of poking about with old rocks.'

'This is different,' she said. 'This is special. It's . . .' She hesitated.

6

'Go on,' he encouraged her.

She looked down at the dragon stone again. 'It's magic,' she said, and grinned shyly.

'You reckon?' He looked pleased.

Franny drew a deep breath. The air was hot and dry in her nose. 'I reckon,' she said. 'This feels special. Like it's the gate to another world.'

'What?'

'I saw this movie, once, where you went through a special door, but it looked like an ordinary door, only when you went through it, POW, you were in another world. Everything was the same. Only different.'

Gerard shook his head. 'Crazy.'

'No. Like you had a pen in your pocket, but when you were in the other world it wasn't a pen any more, it was – ' She searched for an idea. 'It was maybe a dagger.'

Gerard grinned. 'Well, if that's what it takes to make you like this place.'

'Oh, I like it here, but what's it all for?' asked Franny.

'Good.' He put his hand in hers, led her out of the circle. 'I'll tell you later. First, we fix up home.'

Home was a frame tent which they pulled out of the trailer from the back of their battered four-wheel, and assembled with the speed and skill of practised campers. They worked in silence, each knowing the job allocation.

7

'This is *hot*,' said Franny. 'I thought it rained every day in England.'

'You want rain?'

'No.'

'So enjoy the heat.'

Franny brushed aside a bee and worked on.

The man stretched, rubbed his back thoughtfully, winced. 'Getting old,' he muttered, then smiled at Franny. 'That's a record,' he said.

'You reckon?' Her eyes were bright with pleasure.

'I guess,' he said.

'Doesn't count if you didn't time it.'

'It counts if I say so,' he argued. 'So, it's a record.'

'Great!'

Franny rushed into the four-wheel, grabbed a tin shaped like a toad and pulled its head off.

'Ten,' he said.

She counted out ten jelly beans, making sure they were all different flavours.

'Want one?'

'No, thanks. I'll make coffee.'

Franny rationed the jelly beans so that she popped the last one into her mouth just as the man poured a cup of fragrant coffee from the enamel jug. 'I could eat jelly beans all day,' she hinted, with a look at the toad.

'And have your teeth crumble.'

'I guess. Can I have some milk?'

'Help yourself.'

'Milk's got sugar in. Lactose. I could have some more jelly beans instead.'

He grinned at her.

Franny made her lips straight, her usual expression for graciously accepting defeat.

'Gerard?'

'Yes?'

Franny concentrated on pouring the milk. 'Do you suppose . . .'

Gerard waited.

Franny sat down with her back against a wheel of the vehicle. 'I mean, we do all right, just the two of us.' She waited for him to speak. He sipped his coffee. 'You know. I like it. But. Well, do you think Elly might come back, one day?'

Gerard closed his eyes. He had known that the question would come one day, he was just surprised that it had taken his daughter so long to ask it. How long had it been? Nearly two years, since her mother had walked out on them. Franny had been nine then, and had talked about it a lot, but she had never asked this particular question.

'You see, Franny,' he said. 'It's like this . . .'

'Wow!' Franny leaped to her feet. 'Hey! Great! Hey, boy! Here! Come on!'

Gerard looked. A small dog with long sandy hair was bouncing round Franny, grinning up and swiping his tail. Franny fell on him and

9

smothered him. He wriggled, but she had him tight. 'There you go. I've got you, you beauty. Let's just see.'

She found his collar and the small silver disc.

'Towser,' she read. 'What a great name. Let's see where you live.' She turned the disc over, but Towser scrambled away, and with only one free hand Franny couldn't stop him. He bounced away, yelped, grinned, and ran off.

'Here, boy! Come. Come back.'

Gerard sighed, grateful for the escape. But he knew it was only temporary. Franny flopped down next to him. He put his arm around her and held her.

'Tell me,' she said. He groaned silently, inside. He didn't want to talk about him and Elly. Not yet. 'Tell me about the Stonekiller.'

'Oh, right,' said Gerard.

TWO

Gerard's face was open with enthusiasm. 'There's a barrow,' he said. 'Over that way. A burial mound. Very ancient. They used to put kings in them, in ships, sort of preparation for the last long voyage. Well, a team excavated it years ago. Found nothing. There's no one buried there.'

'Yes,' said Franny.

'But, and here's the strange thing. They were going to examine the stone circle as well. That's just as old. Probably the same date. Thousands of years old. But they didn't.'

'Why not?'

'Doesn't say. Except there's supposed to be a curse.' He laughed.

'What sort of curse?'

'It's all nonsense.'

'Tell me anyway.'

'I can't.'

'I'm not a baby. I won't cry.'

'Or have nightmares?'

'No.'

'I still can't tell you.'

Franny scowled.

'Because I don't know,' said Gerard. 'It's just mentioned in the record of the excavation of the barrow.'

'What does it say?'

'It just says that there's a local tradition that anyone who goes into the circle will be captured by Parcel. They're called Parcel's Stones.'

'What?'

'See. It doesn't make sense.'

'It must say more than that.'

'No. Just . . .' He paused. 'Let me try to get this right. Something like . . .' He scratched his head. 'No, it's gone.'

'Gerard!'

He grinned at her. 'Sorry.'

'It's the only interesting thing, and you

forgot it!'

'You'll never be an archaeologist if you think a curse is more interesting than a stone.'

'I don't want to be. Think.'

Gerard sighed. 'Look,' he said, 'all I can remember is that it went something like being caught in Parcel's grip.'

'Huh! And is that why they didn't investigate the stones?'

'No. It was nothing to do with the curse. All the plans were made, but they did nothing. Most of these old circles have been excavated and measured and mapped a hundred times, but there's nothing about this one anywhere, except for a few notes they made when they did the barrow. But even those are no good.'

'So it could have been the curse?' Franny was determined to win.

'No, I guess they just ran out of time. So the drawings and notes are very poor. Inaccurate. Don't even get the number of stones right.'

'How do you know?'

'They give different numbers in different places in the report.'

'So?'

'It's a real find, a real chance. I can make my name with this.'

'Oh.'

'But the first thing is to make sure we know how many stones there are. Coming?'

'Okay.'

Franny slipped her hand into his as they walked back to the stone circle. He gave it a friendly squeeze.

'Might as well make a start,' he said. 'You stand here. We'll call this one number one, all right.'

'Right.'

'Good. How many stones do you think there are?'

She looked round. 'Twenty?'

'Good guess.'

'How many then?'

'The report says twenty-four. Or twenty-two. There used to be more.'

'Count,' said Franny.

'All right. You go this way, I'll go that. We'll meet back here. This stone is number one, remember?'

'Go.'

They paced away from each other, counting. Gerard nodded each time he passed a stone, Franny touched each one, letting her long fingers stroke its rough surface. She shuddered a little at the touch.

'Twenty-three,' she shouted, reaching the finish first.

'Twenty-four,' said Gerard. 'That's funny.'

'I didn't miss any,' said Franny. 'It's twenty-three.'

'Try again,' said Gerard. 'Got to get the same number twice, or it doesn't count.'

Franny grinned. She was used to this obsession with detail and counting. It was how she got her jelly beans.

Franny set off again. 'Twenty-one, twenty-two,' she finished. 'One's disappeared.'

Gerard tried again. Then Franny. Twenty and twenty-four.

'I'll get some chalk,' said Franny. 'Mark them.'

'Another time, perhaps,' said Gerard. 'I'm hot.'

'I'd like to hear about the Stonekiller,' said Franny.

Gerard grinned. His smile was the sort that made you feel good. 'All right,' he agreed. 'I've kept you waiting long enough. Let's go.'

'We'll sit in the centre,' said Franny. 'That's the best place for a story.' She sped into the circle and dropped to the ground next to the carved slab.

'I'm ready,' shouted Franny. 'Come on, Gerard. Let's hear it.'

THREE

The sun was dipping towards the west as Gerard
settled himself to tell the Stonekiller tale. Swal-
lows were wheeling overhead, their wings
spread, tails forked, then diving, swooping low
to catch the early evening insects.

Tall stones cast long shadows.

'When does it get dark?' asked Franny.

'Not for hours yet,' said Gerard. 'Longest day
in about a week.'

A scuffling noise attracted their attention.

'Towser!' called Franny.

The sandy dog thumped its tail against a tall stone, but it stayed away from them.

'Here, boy!'

Towser ignored her.

'That's a weird dog,' said Gerard.

'He's lovely,' said Franny.

'He's a dragon dog.'

'A what?'

'You know. Like a fox terrier, or an otter hound. It sniffs out dragons.'

Franny smacked him lightly. 'What is it really?'

'A spaniel.'

Towser seemed to nod, but Franny wasn't quite sure what he was agreeing with.

'Get on with it,' she said. 'Story.'

'The Stonekiller,' said Gerard. Franny fell silent. Towser looked attentive.

'The excavation notes mentioned an old book, very rare. There's a copy in the university library back home. Apart from that, there's only maybe two other copies known. Here.' He felt in his pocket. 'I've got a page from it.'

'Ripped out?'

'Of course not. Photocopy. Look.' He opened it out.

> Thomas Kych of Herpeton
> Has hidden his secret in his
> Book where none may read –
> It will be well concealed – Be
> Guarded by this advice – Beware
> The wyvern – A man
> Who would find this secret and use
> It must first take heed and
> Delve deep below the wyvern stone far from
> Stone Pond – in Parcel's Stones –
> Take the key from the timbers of
> The buried ship – Nor wake the sleeping
> King

'What does it mean?'

'I think it means there's something here, beneath this stone.'

'A dragon?' said Franny. She stroked the stone nervously. 'I said there was.'

'You may be right,' smiled Gerard. 'But I don't think so.'

'You're boring,' said Franny. 'If it was dragons we could make a wish.'

'Why?'

"Cause they're magic. And you can always make a wish when there's magic.'

Gerard spoke in a soft voice. 'And what would you wish for?'

Franny looked at the paper for a long time, then she folded it and stuffed it into the pocket of her shorts. 'What do you think there is under the stone?'

'A tunnel,' said Gerard.

'Hey?'

'A tunnel.'

'Wow. Why? Where?'

'Remember,' said Gerard. 'The sleeping King.'

'So?'

'I told you. They buried kings in those barrows. In ships. I think there's a tunnel into the barrow.'

'But they dug it up. There wasn't anything.'

'You can't dig everywhere. I think they missed it.'

Franny looked down, as though she could see into the earth.

'That's creepy,' she said.

'More than dragons?'

'Much creepier than dragons. Can we look for the tunnel?'

'Sure.'

'What else does the book say?' asked Franny.

'It tells how, about two hundred years ago, a bit more maybe – I've got the note somewhere in the truck – there was a sudden attack on these stones.'

'Why?'

'The book says they smashed some of them, used them to build houses, but that can't be the reason.'

'Why?' asked Franny.

19

'They'd have smashed the lot. And anyway, there's plenty of clay round here, mostly brick houses.'

'So why did they smash them?' asked Franny.

'Book doesn't say.'

'What does it say?'

Gerard grinned. 'Sorry. Well, this guy, the Stonekiller, he smashed about seven stones in all. They'd tried before, but the stones are just too big, too hard to do much with. Stonekiller, he came up with an idea. What he did was, he built a stack of wood and kindling round one of the stones. Then, he set fire to it, made a giant bonfire.'

'Wow,' said Franny. 'He burned the stone?'

'Yes. Like a witch.'

'Would that smash it?'

'Wait up. Then, when the fire died down and the stone was still real hot, all the villagers threw buckets and buckets of water on it. There's a drawing in the book of the fire and of the people throwing the water. The steam is swirling up like, like . . .' He searched for a picture.

'Like smoke from a dragon's mouth,' said Franny.

'Great, yes.' Gerard beamed at Franny.

'So, then, the heat and the sudden cold weakened the stone. Then, Stonekiller came with a huge hammer and he smashed away at it. It cracked in a thousand places and tumbled to the ground. There's a picture of that as well, with old Stonekiller standing on it, like Goliath on David.'

'Go on,' said Franny.

'Well, it seems he did seven stones, then left the rest. That left twenty-three.'

'Twenty-four,' said Franny. 'Or twenty-two.'

'That's the weirdest thing,' said Gerard, looking round. 'It should be easy enough to count a few stones.'

'So what are you planning to do?' asked Franny.

'Make a proper plan of the site,' said Gerard. 'Count the stones, measure them, measure the area, see how many stones are missing, try to get some idea of what happened here.'

'It's a dragon's home,' said Franny. 'See.' She traced her fingers over the carved figure.

'Round here,' said Gerard, 'they call them wyverns. It says so in the book.'

'It's the same thing,' said Franny.

'Maybe. You concentrate on the dragons,' said Gerard. 'I'll look after the stones.'

'Are we going to dig?'

'No. I'd need permission to do that. Anyway, these circles don't have a lot underneath them, usually.'

'But we're going to look under the dragon stone,' said Franny.

'We'll lift it, have a look,' promised Gerard. 'I guess we'd better eat.'

'We'll start tomorrow,' said Franny.

'Measuring,' said Gerard.

'Looking for dragons,' said Franny.

They stood up. Towser leaped to his feet and sped away.

A boy with sandy hair, the colour of Towser's, watched anxiously. He could see the circle from where he sat on the grass. When Franny and Gerard went into the circle he held his breath, as though frightened that something would happen to them. When Towser looked as though he might trot after them he whispered, 'Stay out. Good dog.' He never took his eyes from them.

The grass was dry beneath his legs. The ground was hot.

'Come on, Towser,' he breathed. 'Come back.' But Towser seemed not to hear.

He stayed tense and anxious until the dog turned and sped towards him. Then he put out his arms and Towser flung himself into them and licked the boy's face all over.

The boy laughed, but he was still not at ease.

He put out his hand and tugged at the collar. He found the silver disc, new and bright in the sun.

'Thomas Ketch,' he read, with satisfaction. 'You're my dog, now. You're not Jack's any more. You're mine.'

Towser rolled on his back.

'Jack's gone away,' said Thomas, not for the first time. 'I'm looking after you now.'

He looked again at the two distant figures. 'So stay out of the stones,' he warned. 'Please.'

Towser grinned.

'I mean it,' said Thomas. 'There'll be trouble. There will, I know it. Stay with me.'

Franny crawled out of her sleeping bag and lay on top of it. Even now that it was dark it was still too hot. She listened carefully. The nib of Gerard's pen scratched the paper as he sat and wrote in the other half of the tent. A small whirring of scaly insects imitated him. Something was squeaking. An owl hooted, softly. Franny knew that its wings were silent and she wondered what sound a dragon's wings would make? Did they fly at night, or in the day time?

'I can't sleep,' she called.

'Come on through.'

Gerard put the cap on his pen and laid it down. 'Come here.'

Franny cuddled him, partly because she liked to feel the comfort of his hug, but more because she knew that he liked it. He had papers spread out in front of him, notebooks, photocopied pages from books, a map.

'What's this?' Franny peered at the map.

'It's here. Look. Here's the stone circle. This is the village.'

Franny followed his finger.

'And this is where we are, right now,' said Gerard.

'There's no tent on the map,' said Franny.

'They weren't expecting us,' said Gerard.

'That's funny,' said Franny. 'It feels as though they were. What's this?' Her finger found a blue circle.

'Stone Pond,' read Gerard. 'Hey, that's on your photocopy.'

'Where is it?'

'Just down the lane and in a dip.'

Franny let her head fall against his shoulder. 'Do you have to do this work?'

'Yes. There's nothing about these stones. If I make a good report it will help me to get a better job. Get anywhere else. Get you into a good school.'

Franny scowled. 'Don't want to go to school. Want to stay with you.'

'When summer's over we're going home. You start in Fall.'

'Where?'

'Depends. On this report. On the stones. So give me a break, huh?'

'Gerard?'

'Yes.'

'If Elly wanted to come back, would you let her?'

'Is that what you'd like?'

'Only if you do.'

'Well, I guess it would be good.'

'I miss her.'

'Yes.'

'Sometimes, it's like there's something wrong with me.'

Gerard hugged her. 'There's nothing wrong with you, Franny.'

'I know. It just feels like there is. Like there's something broken. Or something missing.'

Gerard tried hard not to speak.

Franny buried her face in his shirt. 'It's like a . . . a . . . headache, or something. I wish there was a pill I could take, to make it better.'

'Yes.'

'Why did she leave?'

Gerard kept his face turned away from Franny so she could not see him. 'All kinds of reasons.'

'Was it her fault?'

'You know, Franny, when that sort of thing happens, there's usually faults on both sides.'

'What did you do wrong?'

'Time you were asleep, I think.'

Franny yawned. 'I'm not tired.'

'We'll see.'

He carried her back through into her part of the tent, settled her on the sleeping bag, drawing a light sheet over her.

'Good night, Fran.'

''Night, Gerard.'

The insects whirred.

'Oh, Gerard.'

'Yes?'

'Tomorrow.'

'Yes?'

'I'll help you.'

'I'd like that.'

'We'll count the stones again. Properly this time.'

'If they let us.'

'Good night.'

Gerard stepped outside the tent. The last light was dying and the night drew its black wing over the sky.

FOUR

'I need you to hold this,' said Gerard. 'Keep it right up to where the stone meets the ground, on the outside edge.'

Franny held the end of the tape measure while Gerard backed away from her.

'I reckon the wyvern stone is dead in the centre of the circle,' he predicted.

Franny felt the tape tugging at her fingers as Gerard unwound it.

'Right,' he called. 'That's twenty feet. Come on over.'

Franny went over to meet him and put the tape down again where he had marked the ground with a wooden peg.

'You're not going straight,' she warned him.

Gerard veered off, crossed the wyvern stone. 'Thirty feet,' he called, then stopped again. 'That's forty, to the outside of the stone.'

Franny trotted up to him again, put the tape on the second wooden peg.

'Exactly sixty feet,' said Gerard. He pulled the tape from her and wound it up into its battered case.

'It'll take all day to measure round the edge,' said Franny. She sat, cross-legged on the ground, feeling the warmth of the sun on her face.

Gerard wagged a finger at her. 'We don't need to.'

'Why?'

'You can pace it out.'

'That's no good. I'll lose count, or my strides will be different lengths.'

'Let's try.'

Gerard measured Franny's pace. 'Two feet,' he said. 'More or less. Try to keep it that long.'

Franny snorted.

'Start here. And here, write it down when you've finished, but don't tell me.'

Franny shrugged her shoulders, but she set

off, counting carefully.

Gerard leaned against the stone she started from and took out a pocket calculator.

Franny touched each stone as she passed it.

Gerard grinned at her as she got back to him. 'Jot it down.'

Franny scribbled a number in a little notebook.

'Right,' said Gerard. 'Within five paces. If I'm right I get ten jelly beans. If I'm wrong you get twenty. Deal?'

'Deal,' said Franny.

Gerard looked at his calculator. 'Ninety-five paces,' he said.

Franny squealed. 'You watched me. You counted.'

'No. How many?'

'Ninety-seven.'

'Ten jelly beans for me.'

'How did you do it?'

'Magic.'

'How?'

'I guessed.'

'How, Gerard? Before I get mad.'

'All right. Look. From the edge to the centre is thirty feet, right?'

'Right.'

'So, if I times two by three point one four seven, times thirty –' He tapped in the numbers. 'I get one hundred and eighty-eight, point eight two.'

'So?'

'So, call that one hundred ninety.'

'Okay.'

'One hundred ninety feet. You pace two feet each time, so divide by two. You get ninety-five. Ninety-five paces.'

Franny bit her lip. 'Why?'

'Don't know. It always works. Any circle. Two times three point one four seven, times the distance from the edge to the centre. Gives you the measurement round the edge.'

'That's weird.'

'I guess. Let's get these stones counted properly.'

'It doesn't matter,' said Franny.

'But it does matter,' said Gerard. 'I'll write this up. Publish it, in a journal. I have to get it right. Someone could come and check.'

There was a sudden rustling in the dry grass. Franny looked down. A ribbon of black, painted with vivid gold diamonds lay crumpled against the stone. She put her hand down to touch it.

'Don't!' Gerard pushed her away.

'Ow!'

'What?' Gerard tried to catch Franny as she fell.

'You hurt me.'

The ribbon writhed away swiftly.

'What was it?' she asked.

'Viper.'

'What?' Franny rubbed her knee.

'Snake. Poisonous.'

'No poisonous snakes in England,' said Franny. 'Everyone knows that.'

'These are. They probably couldn't kill you, but they do a lot of damage. Make you very ill. And, of course, the smaller you are, the worse it is. Can't kill a man. Might kill a small girl. That's the strangest thing.'

'What?'

'The book said there were a lot round here, for some reason. I didn't believe it.'

'Why?' asked Franny.

'How's your knee?'

'I'll mend. Why are there lots round here?'

'Something to do with the dragons, it said. They come out when it's hot. Usually they hibernate during the winter, but they can even come out then. I think there were a lot more of them in England once than there are now, but with the new methods of farming and with the poisons they use on the land there are fewer and fewer. But it looks like there are still plenty round here.'

'Why?'

'They have a diamond shape on their backs. They're also known as adders, but the old name for them, the one in the book, is wyverns.'

'Like the dragons?'

'That's it.'

'So the dragons aren't real? They're just snakes with legs?'

'Did it look like a snake with legs?'

'No.'

'No. So be careful.'

'Let's eat,' said Franny.

'Okay.'

'Then can I have the afternoon off?'

Gerard took her hand and they walked back to the tent together. 'Had enough of being an archaeologist?'

'It's too hot. I want to go to that pond.'

'No swimming.'

'Can I paddle?'

'I guess. If there's any water.'

'Why?'

'Been a long drought. Ponds dry up.'

The pond lay at the bottom of the hill. It had a dark heart, and a reddy-brown edge, wide and regular.

Franny broke into a trot and sped down the hill. The small dog appeared on the other side.

'Here, boy!' called Franny. 'Towser!'

He wagged his tail, let his mouth hang open in a wide grin, and stayed put.

The dark heart was the small circle of water, the red ring the outer circle of baked mud.

'Wow.' Franny stepped on to the hard mud. 'Some drought.'

The mud was cracked and crazed like an old plate.

'It's nearly all gone,' she said.

It was silent, lonely standing where the water had once stood. Franny felt a prickle of fear. She shook herself and started to jog round, to get rid of the eerie feeling. 'I know,' she said to herself. She ran to the edge, where the red mud met the green fringe. She scratched a deep mark in the mud to indicate her starting place. Then she paced out the perimeter of the pond. Towser ran ahead of her, keeping his distance. 'Ninety-three, ninety-four, ninety-five, ninety-six, ninety-seven.' Her foot landed on her mark. Franny whistled, sat down, looked around the pond and shook her head. 'That's the strangest thing,' she murmured. 'Exactly the same size as the stone circle.' She sat and stared long and hard at the pool of water in the centre until her eyes hurt and her head was swimming with the heat.

Finding a shady, if not exactly cool spot beneath a tree, Franny took out her piece of paper with the strange inscription.

> Thomas Kych of Herpeton
> Has hidden his secret in his
> Book where none may read –
> It will be well concealed – Be
> Guarded by this advice – Beware
> The wyvern – A man
> Who would find this secret and use
> It must first take heed and

> Delve deep below the wyvern stone far from
>   Stone Pond – in Parcel's Stones –
> Take the key from the timbers of
>   The buried ship – Nor wake the sleeping
>   King

She read it over and over, but it made no sense at all. The empty feeling in her stomach made Franny decide to give up and go back to Gerard. The writing didn't mean anything. She folded the paper, looked up at the pond. But there was something, there must be. The pond was exactly the same size as the stone circle. Why? Her stomach complained, loudly. Franny glanced down at the folded paper. She blinked, looked again. A sudden excitement seized her. Yes. She beat her fists against the tree in pleasure. It was there all the time and no one had seen it. But Franny had. She'd worked it out. This would take some thinking out. She had to take her time, work out a plan. She stuffed the paper into her pocket and ran up the hill. Towser watched her disappear.

FIVE

The scent of the fresh coffee woke Franny, and for just a moment she forgot that Elly had left them and that they were in a foreign country. She expected to see her mother and share breakfast, the three of them.

Then she opened her eyes, saw the filtered sunlight through the sides of the tent and her stomach flipped over. She felt dizzy, a little sick.

'Breakfast!' called Gerard.

'Coming.' Franny managed to keep her sadness from her voice, but her eyes let her down. She rubbed her face against her pillow, letting the tears soak into the fabric.

When it had been kind enough to hide her misery, Franny rewarded the pillow by punching it hard. Hitting it made her feel better, a little better anyway.

'I want to look under the wyvern stone today,' she told Gerard.

'All right.'

'After breakfast.'

'Later. We've got to go to the village first.'

'I don't want to.'

'Got to. We're out of everything.'

'You go. I'll wait here.'

'You get washed and dressed. We'll go in about a quarter of an hour. I'll clear the breakfast things.'

Franny gave in more or less gracefully. She tucked a small notebook and a stub of pencil and Gerard's calculator in the pocket of her shorts, and she made sure she had her piece of paper. Just in case. 'I'll count the wyverns,' she said.

The path into the village was downhill most of the way, then up just a little towards the end, so that the manor house, and the church next to it, stood on a mound on low ground.

The Manor was gaunt and grey, blind where the windows had been boarded up. Franny was

36

glad she was outside. She imagined dark passageways and echoing empty rooms. It was disturbing. And somehow the wyverns made it even more creepy.

She pulled herself together and got on with her task.

Franny carefully counted the wyverns – two on the gateposts, one on the pub sign. She made notes of them. She failed to notice the one that perched on the steeple as a weather vane, because of the huge man in black skirts who stood in the churchyard and waved to them. His black hair and beard gave him a menacing appearance that was at odds with the broad smile and friendly wave.

'He gives me the creeps,' said Franny.

They stood below a statue on the village green.

'She's weird,' said Gerard.

'I think she looks fine,' said Franny.

They read the inscription on the plinth.

JANE GWYER
Born 1743
*who, for twelve years was Mistress
of Wivern Manor, until her sudden
Disappearance in 1781. Mild of Manner,
yet she was Strong of Purpose, her
Desire always to Right wrongs. She
was Even-handed to Creatures of
Whatsoever Estate, Conscientious in*

her Duty, Faithful and Obedient as a
Daughter, Condescending to
the Poor,
unmoved by the Pretentions of
the Great.
All Creatures of the Hearth and
Beasts of the Wild were her
Friends and knew no Fear where
she was, or where
She Is Now.

'What does it mean?' asked Franny. She looked into the young face of the statue for an answer.

'There's another dragon,' said Gerard, pointing to a small serpent carved next to the inscription.

'Wyvern,' Franny corrected him, noting it in her book. She remembered the wyvern stone and made a note of that one before she forgot.

The village shop had most of the things they wanted, but no fresh coffee and no jelly beans.

Franny was horrified.

'What do kids eat?'

'There's jelly babies,' suggested the lady. 'Are they the same thing?'

'We'll try them, please,' said Gerard.

'Ugh,' said Franny, biting the head off one. 'They're terrible.' But she stuffed the bag into the pocket of her shorts.

'Thank you,' said Gerard. 'That's all.'

The lady gave him his change and they left the

shop, making the bell over the door clang.

'What am I going to do with you?' asked Gerard.

'What?'

'The lady was being helpful, and you were just rude.'

'Was I?'

'Yes. I could see she was cross with you.'

Franny ran back, flung the door open, clanging the bell.

'If you make it worse,' muttered Gerard.

Franny came banging out, and Gerard thought the bell would lose its clapper. She was sucking a lolly, its stick poking out of her mouth.

'Well?' he asked, grimly.

'I said sorry,' Franny mumbled through her lolly. 'And she gave me this.'

Gerard grabbed her, swept her off her feet, hugged her and gave her a kiss.

Franny beat him with her fists. 'Get off. Get off, now, Gerard!'

'I could eat you sometimes,' said Gerard.

'I'm warning you. Quick. Before someone sees us.'

Gerard put her down. Franny ran well away from him and walked right ahead until they were clear of the village and on the path back up to their tent. Then she lagged her steps until he was level with her.

'You're so embarrassing,' she complained.

Gerard grinned.

'Can we do the wyvern stone now?'

'Can you wait till after lunch?'

'I guess.'

They passed the stone circle. Franny darted round the stones, weaving in and out, but not all the way round.

'I'll wait,' Gerard offered. But Franny stopped.

'No,' she said. 'I don't want to run all the way round.'

She linked hands with him and they walked back to the tent.

While Gerard fixed lunch Franny organised her plan. Opening her notebook, she listed the wyverns she had counted. Then she copied out the writing from the photocopy. She took great care over this, using a double page of the notebook, with the writing going across the middle. She studied this carefully until Gerard called her.

'What do you think you'll find under the wyvern stone?'

Franny thought. 'The tunnel.'

'And?'

'A map. Or another book.'

Gerard nodded.

'What do you think?' she asked.

'I don't know. I want there to be a tunnel, into the barrow. But I daren't hope.'

'I just want to see,' she said. 'You know.'

'Yes.'

Gerard chewed his sandwich. Then, 'Franny, are you holding out on me?'

Franny looked away.

'What's going on?'

'I'll tell you tonight,' she promised him. 'When we've looked under the wyvern stone.'

'Come on, then.' Gerard stood up, brushed the crumbs from his clothes. 'Let's lift the stone.'

SIX

The stone was chipped on one edge.

'Look,' said Gerard. 'It was lifted not long ago. These marks are fresh. There's no moss or lichen on them.'

'Someone's been looking before us,' said Franny.

'You might be right,' said Gerard. He slid the end of his crowbar into the side of the wyvern stone. 'This is hot work,' he said.

The circle seemed to trap the sun and hold its heat. There was no breeze. Gerard's face gleamed with his efforts. His shirt clung to his back.

'I'll help.'

'Please. Stay back. If you trap your fingers . . .'

He tried a better place, levered the bar and felt the stone yield.

'Getting there,' he said.

He shifted the crowbar, easing the stone higher.

'Don't damage it,' warned Franny.

Gerard grimaced. 'It's me that's getting damaged.'

The stone fell back, groaning.

Gerard slumped to the ground, mopped his brow and sighed.

'Come on, Gerard.'

He grinned at Franny. 'I'm glad you're not my boss.'

'Sorry.'

There was a movement in the grass.

'Franny!'

'Yes?'

'Don't move.'

She followed his eyes.

A bright viper slid past her foot. It crossed the wyvern stone, hesitated, stopped, enjoying the concentrated heat of the sun on the stone, then slid away.

'It's beautiful,' said Franny.

'I'd have thought they were timid,' said Gerard. 'Not like that.'

'It belongs here,' said Franny. 'It doesn't care about us.'

Gerard watched it disappear.

'Come on,' Franny urged him.

He put the curved end of the crowbar back against the rim of the wyvern stone, braced himself, pushed, and suddenly the stone lifted and fell to one side, as though it weighed nothing at all.

'Wow!' said Gerard.

'The viper did it,' said Franny.

Gerard wiped a hand over his wet forehead. 'Not from where I'm standing,' he said.

Franny bent down to look into the hole where the stone had lain. She put her hand in.

'Bricks,' she said. 'Lining the sides.'

Gerard shone a torch into the hole. 'There's a tunnel. It goes off at the side.' He ran his finger over the bricks. 'But these are much newer than a ship burial would be. Someone's kept this tunnel safe. It's been worked on since.'

Franny dropped down into the hole.

'Careful.'

'It's not deep.' Franny's voice was excited. 'I can get into the tunnel.'

Gerard handed her the torch. 'How far does it go?'

Franny shone the torch. 'Only a few yards.'

Her voice gave away her disappointment.

Franny crouched down. She stepped into the tunnel.

'Be careful.'

Franny's hands searched the rubble of the collapsed tunnel, trying to find a gap, a way through. 'Nothing,' she called. 'It's blocked. There's no way.'

'Come on out.'

Franny's head popped up from the hole.

'Is it any good?' she asked.

Gerard shrugged. 'Might be. Unless we excavate we won't know.'

'Does it go to the King?'

Gerard's face showed his frustration and disappointment. 'I don't know. It might. Or it might be fairly new. No one's ever looked.'

'Is it good for your work?'

'It's hard to say. It means a lot more work, and it might be all for nothing.'

'I hope it's good,' said Franny, scrambling out. 'Thanks.'

'There's one thing, though.'

'What?'

'It was cool down there.'

'Listen,' said Gerard. 'You're not to come back here on your own.'

'I won't.'

'Or ever to go in anything like that without me.'

'I know. I'm not stupid.'

'Just as long as I know.'

'Anyway, it's eerie down there.'

'Makes no difference. I'll put the stone back.'

Franny helped him. It slid back into place with a sigh. 'I'm going to the pond,' she said.

'Will you take the things back to the tent?' asked Gerard, handing her the torch and the crowbar.

'I'll look after them,' she said, not liking to tell him a direct lie. 'And I'll have another look around. See what I can find.'

'Don't forget to put it in your notebook,' he teased her. 'I may want to write it up in my report.'

'Sure.'

'Back about five, please. No, wait.'

'Yes?'

'Make it six. In the village. We need some things from the shop.'

Franny pulled a face.

'And I'll buy you an ice cream.'

'Great!'

Franny took the things and ran off. Gerard turned his attention to careful measurements of the circle.

On her way past the tent Franny grabbed a small plastic bottle of fizzy drink for later, but she didn't put down the torch or the crowbar. She ran down the hill, over the stile and skidded to a halt on the rim of Stone Pond.

The edge of the mud that marked the old limit of the water was a fairly sharp line of grass and ferns. Franny perched on this, sitting on the green border with her feet on the red earth. She opened her notebook, turned to the page with the copied inscription on it.

> Thomas Kych of Herpeton
> Has hidden his secret in his
> Book where none may read –
> It will be well concealed – Be
> Guarded by this advice – Beware
> The wyvern – A man
> Who would find this secret and use
> It must first take heed and
> Delve deep below the wyvern stone far from
> Stone Pond – in Parcel's Stones –
> Take the key from the timbers of
> The buried ship – Nor wake the sleeping
> King

She folded the book over so that only the left-hand side of the page was showing.

> Thomas Kych
> Has hidden his
> Book where
> It will be well
> Guarded by
> The wyvern

Who would find
It must first
Delve deep below
Stone Pond
Take the key from the
The buried
King

Franny grinned. 'And you can't delve deep below a pond,' she said quietly. 'Unless the pond's dried up.'

She took off her shoes and socks and walked towards the small circle of water in the centre of the dried mud.

The water was warm at the edge, growing cooler as she neared the centre. Her toes sank into the wetter mud beneath the surface. Small bubbles rose through the murky water. Franny enjoyed the cool, sticky feeling of pulling her feet up from the bottom.

She stopped near the centre, gripped the crowbar and hesitated. She went on. Her foot felt something smooth and hard beneath it. She stepped forward. Now she was exactly in the centre of Stone Pond and she could feel a smooth solid surface beneath her feet, slippery, yet firm.

She rubbed the soles of her feet against it, feeling the mud clear. There was a ridge, interrupting the smoothness. The more mud she cleared the more obvious was the pattern. She could not read it, but she could guess. Her hair prickled on the back of her neck as she imagined the wyvern beneath her feet, twin to the one carved on the wyvern stone in the circle.

How long had this beast lain hidden? And who had put it there? Franny remembered visiting a dam once, with Elly and Gerard. They had explained that the lake on the far side had once been a valley, with trees and houses, but that the dam had flooded it. Perhaps this had once been a dip in the landscape and someone had flooded it after they had put the wyvern stone in place?

Franny felt that the mud was nearly all clear now. She could make out the round rim of the stone. The water was just above her ankles. Looking back at the old line of the bank she was surprised to see that the slopes of red mud ran up, so that the rim of the pond, when full, was way over the top of her head. Normally, this stone would be ten, more, feet below the surface. No wonder it had been hidden for so long.

Franny tucked the torch into her waistband, stooped and stepped aside. She fitted the end of the crowbar into the rim of the stone, just as she had seen Gerard do. The stone lifted with no effort at all. The water sloshed around and drained down, with a rather rude noise that made Franny giggle. She looked round and realised that the bottom of the pond sloped up slightly towards the middle, so that she now stood, looking down at a hole, with a stone to one side, surrounded by a ring of water, bounded by the dry red mud. Like a target, green then red, then brown, then the black hole at the centre.

The stone half covered the hole. Franny pushed it.aside. She shone the torch down. It was just like the one in the stone circle. A brick-lined drop, like a well, turned into a tunnel, about five feet down.

She knew she had to go and get Gerard. She had found it. It was her discovery, now she could let him in on it. A movement behind her made her jump. Then she squealed as something hit her legs. Towser brushed past her and leaped into the hole.

'Come out!' she shouted. 'Here, Towser. Come on out!'

Nothing happened.

Franny remembered Gerard's warning and started to move away, then she heard a whimpering noise.

'Are you all right?'

The whimpering stopped.

Knowing that she was doing wrong, Franny flicked on the torch, lowered herself into the hole, took one last look at the bright sunlight and went into the tunnel.

Almost immediately she came to a dead end. Towser was waiting for her there. Her fingers found a wooden surface. Her torch revealed a door, wide and short, with long iron braces attaching it to sturdy hinges. The iron braces went halfway across the door and were beaten into the shape of wyverns with gaping mouths.

'Let's go.' She took Towser's collar in her fingers. He twisted round and scratched at the door.

'Well,' said Franny. 'While we're down here . . .'

Franny moved the torch over the door. It discovered an iron ring. She gripped it, lifted, twisted. A latch lifted on the other side. Franny pushed. The door swung open, silently. Towser darted through. Franny took a deep breath, stepped after him. The door swung shut.

A woman looked out of her window and saw Gerard searching anxiously round the village. He walked past the pub.

She was in bed, and held herself in a strange way, fearing that if she should relax then the pain would come back again.

She was thin, tired, always tired.

The boy next to her, sitting on her bed, tried to talk as though nothing was wrong.

'You should go out and play,' she told him. 'You shouldn't be sitting up here with me. Not in the summer.'

'Summer's all right,' he said. 'But it's too hot. I like it better here.'

There was something she wanted to say, but it was hard.

'You and your dad need a holiday,' she said. 'You could go away for a bit if I went back into the hospital, just for a few days.'

'We'll all go, together,' he said. 'When you're better.'

She sighed, lay back and looked at the low ceiling.

The lady in the shop hadn't seen Franny. Gerard tried outside. He looked up to a creaky sign which marked the Green Dragon pub. Its paint was flaking off; the boards were warped and twisted and hung over the legend

L. S. Caton, licensed to sell retail beer, wines and spirits for consumption on or off the premises.

She couldn't be in there.

The evening sun washed the colour from the windows and splashed it on the walls and floor of the church.

'Franny!' Gerard's call broke the fragile silence.

'Not here.'

The deep voice made Gerard turn round. The huge man in the black skirts stepped out from the shadows.

'I've been here all afternoon. There's no one here.'

He was several inches taller even than Gerard, and broad, strong.

'I've seen you in the village,' said Weever.

'I'm an archaeologist,' said Gerard. 'My daughter's gone missing.'

'Long?'

'Since lunch.'

Weever tugged at the ends of his hair. 'Any idea?'

'Counting wyverns,' said Gerard.

'That'll take a long time round here.'

'We lifted the wyvern stone,' said Gerard.

'Did you, now?' The huge man looked interested. 'And what did you find?'

'A brick shaft. A collapsed tunnel.'

Weever looked pleased.

'I'd better get on,' said Gerard.

'Where?'

Gerard admitted to himself what he had been trying not to think about.

'Stone Pond,' he said.

'It's all right,' said the man, when he saw the anxiety on Gerard's face. 'It's dried up, nearly. Only a few inches deep. She can't come to any harm.'

'I'd better go there.'

'I'll come with you.'

'There's no need.'

'It's my job,' he said. 'I'm the vicar. Sorry,' he added. 'We haven't met. My name's Weever.' He held out his hand. His cuff slid back and revealed a snake, tattooed on his forearm, writhing.

Gerard did not take his hand. He stared at the tall man.

'What's the matter?' asked Weever.

'Weever?' said Gerard.

'That's right.'

'That's the Stonekiller. Stonekiller Weever.'

'Who's that?'

SEVEN

The door swung shut and Franny was in darkness. Her hands trembled. What if the door stuck and she could not get out? She shone her torch round. She was in a small round room, with brick walls, no windows, and a high ceiling. If she stood in the centre of the room she could touch the walls all around her. She could not reach the ceiling. The floor was laid with smooth flagstones.

Apart from Franny and Towser, the room was

completely empty.

'Now look what you've done,' she said.

Towser licked her leg.

Franny was relieved to find nothing dangerous beyond the door, but disappointed to reach a dead end. She was confident now that the door would open again when she tried it. Everything was so ordinary, so safe. She paused for a moment to enjoy the sensation of being in the small space with the dry, rough walls and the heavy door.

'Ah, well,' she said. 'I'd better go.'

Despite her conviction that the door would open, she felt a momentary thrill of anxiety as she put her hand to the iron ring. She remembered Gerard's warning about going into a closed space. Not the first time he had told her. She might get trapped. She might suffocate. She might never be found and starve to death. All these warnings leaped into her head as she held her breath and twisted the iron ring.

The door opened smoothly and easily. Franny breathed out.

'Come on, Towser.'

She stepped through the door and found herself in a larger room, with high windows, a stone floor, and the sound of something roaring and crashing outside. Towser slipped after her.

In the centre of the room, at a large desk, sat a boy in a long, grey cloak. His head was down; he was scratching at a thick piece of paper with a long quill.

The door slammed behind Franny. The boy jumped, looked up. He blinked, laid down his quill, making a blot on the paper, and rubbed his eyes. His sleeve fell back and Franny saw a purple mark on his forearm in the shape of a wyvern.

'Ah,' said the boy. 'You've come, then.'

Gerard saw Franny's footprints in the mud at the water's rim. He saw the flat, round stone, traced the shape of the wyvern with his fingers. He hardly dared to look at the gaping hole in the earth.

'Franny,' he called.

The noise echoed back to him.

He lowered himself into the opening, squeezing to get his large body where Franny's small one had fitted so easily, and where Towser had slipped so quickly.

'Franny! Are you there?'

He ducked his head into the darkness.

'Oh, Franny,' he whispered. 'If you only knew how much I hate being locked in.'

His fingers felt ahead of him and he moved forward with stooped back.

It was a lovely room. The light was soft and warm and Franny felt she could almost taste it after the gloom of the tunnel. The walls were smooth and curved, the ceiling was high, wooden, and painted in the liveliest and gayest colours. Tall, narrow windows broke the walls at regular intervals.

Franny stepped forward, unafraid.

The boy put down his quill pen and came over to her. He took both of her hands in his and held them. He smiled. 'Thomas,' he said. 'It's good to see you.'

'Franny.'

He let go of her hands and went back to the desk. 'And how do you spell that?'

Franny was too overwhelmed to be surprised and she answered his questions as though she had applied for a library ticket. 'Eff. Ar. Ay. En. En. Wye.'

He tickled his ear with the feather. 'That's a new one on me.'

'Short for Frances.'

'Ah, yes.' He made a note of it. 'Frances.'

'I love your ceiling.'

'Do you? Do you, really? I'm so glad.' He took her hand again and they looked up together. Wyverns circled over their heads against a clear blue sky. 'All gone, now, though.'

'Eh?'

'The wyverns. All gone.'

'What happened?'

'It was all a very long time ago.'

Franny waited for him to answer her question. 'Are you hungry'? he asked.

'No.'

'Thirsty?'

'Um . . .'

'I could get you some beer. Or a glass of wine.'
Franny giggled.

'Or perhaps you've had some wine already?'

'I'm not drunk.' Franny pulled herself together.

'Ah.'

'I'm sorry. Thank you. Have you got any coffee?'
Thomas looked pleased. 'Any what?'

'Coffee?'

He grabbed the quill and dipped it in the ink.
'How do you spell that?'

'See. Oh. Eff. Eff. Ee. Ee. I guess you haven't
got any.'

'No.'

Franny went over to a window and peered
through. She felt sick and pulled her head
straight back in.

Thomas looked out.

Franny stepped back from the opening.

'Something wrong?'

'Where are we? What is this place?'

'Stone Tower.'

The full strangeness of what had happened
suddenly hit Franny.

Thomas led her over to the desk, sat her in his
chair and poured her a glass of something red
and sparkling.

Franny sipped it. Drank a little. Drank it

down. It was light, faintly sweet, refreshing.

'Was that wine?'

'Not really. Grape juice.' Thomas sniffed. 'Sometimes it ferments just a little and then you . . .'

Franny felt much better.

'This is a pit, underground,' she said.

Thomas nodded. 'From one point of view.'

'So what's that out there?'

'That's the sea,' said Thomas.

'I know that.'

'Oh.' He shrugged, smiled. 'Is this a game?'

'What is this place?' she asked again. 'And what are you?'

'Look again.' He took her to the window. Franny was prepared this time for what she saw.

They stood, high above a rocky coastline. Far beneath them, waves crashed on the shore, sending up feathers of spume. This was the roaring noise Franny had first heard when she stepped into the room. Out to sea – it was easier for Franny to look into the distance because it stopped her feeling dizzy when she looked straight down – out to sea, long ships, three, four, at least, sliced through the high waves. Their curved sides sent the spindrift churning behind them. Their wide, square sails bellied out in the wind. And their prows ate the waves – wyverns' heads with gaping mouths.

Franny kept her hands firmly on the brick

lining of the thick stone walls. But even had she wanted to jump out the window was too narrow for her to get through.

She forced herself to look down. Franny had been in high buildings in America, but never one that felt as tall as this. Partly it was an illusion, because the high, slim tower was perched on a cliff, so the distance to the sea was greater than the height of the building. Partly it was that the tower stood alone, not surrounded by other high buildings like the offices in New York. But more than anything it was the great stone slabs from which it was made, and the old carvings and the narrow windows. Nothing so old should be so tall.

Franny looked down. The tower was like a pencil, standing on its end. She felt as though it might topple over any second. Franny felt her sickness returning. She closed her eyes.

'Sorry,' said Thomas. He laid a hand on her shoulder. 'I'm used to it, of course. But it must be a shock.'

Franny nodded. She looked again. Seagulls circled below them.

'Come to the other side. That's easier to get used to.'

There was a sudden flurry and Towser leaped up at the window. Franny screamed and grabbed him before he could wriggle through the gap and plunge down on to the distant rocks.

They fell backwards in a heap and Towser licked her face.

Thomas gaped at them.

Franny struggled to her feet.

'I'm sorry,' she said. 'He's all right, really.'

Thomas was rubbing his eyes.

'Are you all right?' asked Franny.

Thomas ran to a shelf and pulled down a book.

'He's not fierce,' said Franny.

Towser sat, with a long pink tongue hanging out of the side of his mouth. One of his long ears had flopped on to the top of his head.

Thomas flicked through the thick pages of the book.

'Yes,' he said. 'Yes! Look!'

He hurried across the room, nearly tripping on his long gown.

'See!'

Franny peered at the book. Towser jumped up into her arms to look with her.

Thomas was pointing to a drawing of a dog. A small, sandy dog, with long ears and flowing hair. A spaniel. Beneath the drawing were the words:

DRAGON DOG.

Towser grinned at it.

'Oh, no,' said Franny.

EIGHT

'Where did you get the Dragon Dog?' asked Thomas.

'He's a spaniel,' said Franny.

Thomas shook his head.

Towser shook his head, too.

'Where am I?' asked Franny, feeling foolish.

'I've got to find out all about you,' said Thomas. 'And write it down.'

'No way,' said Franny. 'You answer my questions first.'

'Oh,' said Thomas.

'Are you a monk?' asked Franny.

'No,' he laughed. 'Not at all. Why?'

'Your clothes are funny.'

Thomas smiled. 'You might think so,' he said. 'But I must tell you, that here, people do not walk about with their arms and legs showing, as you do.'

Franny looked at her shorts and T-shirt. She had never thought of herself in this way before – as a foreigner might see her. It was peculiar.

'What are you, then?'

'A scholar.'

'My dad's a scholar.'

They reached the opposite window. Franny took a deep breath and looked out.

This side of the tower faced the land, so the drop was about a quarter of the height from the other side. And it showed that the tower was attached to the corner of a large castle.

'Is that how you came here?' asked Thomas. He scurried back to the desk and wrote 'scholar'.

'Do you write everything down?'

'Most things. Otherwise they fly away.'

'What's going on down there?'

'How did your father break through the gate? And why did he send you? He should have come himself. And where did you find the Dragon Dog?'

Towser cocked his head to one side.

'Is it a castle? I thought all castles were ruins.'

An ox cart approached the gate, far below them. With a creaking and a grating a drawbridge was lowered and the cart drove across. The drawbridge was raised again.

'What good would a ruined castle be?' asked Thomas.

Franny put her hand in her pocket and pulled out the bag of jelly babies. She popped one into her mouth, then realising she had been rude, offered the bag to Thomas. He looked carefully, nervously.

'They're all right,' she said. 'Not as good as jelly beans, though.'

Thomas took a red jelly baby out. 'Is it magic?'

Franny laughed. She popped another into her mouth.

Thomas looked horrified. 'You really eat them?'

'Sure.'

He turned his round and round in his fingers. 'How do you turn them to jelly?'

'You buy them.'

Thomas put it into a little box.

'They're all right,' said Franny. She ate another one.

'We don't eat babies here,' he said.

Franny laughed and stuffed the bag back into her pocket.

'What do you study?' she asked.

'The wyverns.'

'Have you got some? Here?'

Thomas looked surprised.

'Can I see one?'

Thomas ran across to his desk and scribbled furiously on the piece of paper.

'What are you writing?'

'I just want to make sure that I don't forget.'

'What?'

'That you think we have the wyverns.'

'Don't you?'

'You do.'

'Who?'

'You.'

'Me?'

'Yes.'

'No.'

'No?'

'Where?'

Thomas pointed to the door that Franny had come in through. 'That's where the wyverns live. That's why you've got a Dragon Dog.'

Franny hitched herself up on to the edge of the desk and dangled a leg.

'You've got that wrong,' she said. 'There's no wyverns through there. Unless . . .'

'Yes?' Thomas asked eagerly.

'Unless you mean like those.' Franny pointed to the painted wyverns circling the ceiling.

Thomas scribbled furiously.

'What happened to them?' he asked, lifting

his head.

Franny shrugged. 'Search me.'

'What?'

'I don't know.' Then she had an idea. 'There's this,' she said. She took out the paper with the inscription.

Thomas seized it. He read it carefully. 'Can I have this?'

'No.'

'Then I must copy it.'

'Okay.'

'Please?'

'I said yes.'

When he had finished Thomas looked up, gave Franny the paper back.

'What's the big deal?' she asked.

'I,' he said grandly, 'am Thomas Kych. The Wyvern Master.'

Towser ran across to the door they had come in through and started sniffing and scratching at it.

'What's up, Towser?' asked Franny.

She put her hand out to open the door but Towser pushed her away.

'What's the matter?'

Towser whined and scratched.

Franny thought she perhaps heard a small clatter on the other side.

Thomas called across to her. 'How do you spell "Towser"?'

Franny told him and Towser trotted over to them.

'Are there wyverns here?' asked Franny.

'Now that you've come, with the Dragon Dog, there will be,' said Thomas. And he clenched his fists in delight.

'And can they make wishes come true?'

'They *are* a wish come true,' he said. 'Why? Did you have a special wish?'

'No,' said Franny.

'That's odd,' said Thomas.

'Why?'

'Because everyone else has got a special wish. You must live in a wonderful land where there is no need for special wishes.'

He noticed the way that Franny turned her head and brushed her arm against her face, but he did not say any more about wishes.

'Shall we get a wyvern?' he asked.

'Oh, yes!'

Towser jumped up and licked his face.

'Yes,' said Thomas. 'We need you as well.'

Gerard found the handle of the door and turned it.

'Franny,' he said, in a soft voice. 'Are you there?'

He held his breath as he stepped through. Striking a match he smelled the swift flare and then looked round. Disappointed to find an empty room, he was also relieved not to find

Franny lying on the floor. He examined the walls carefully, looking for another door. The wooden door swung shut behind him and his match burned out.

Gerard struck another, satisfied himself that Franny wasn't there and that she couldn't have gone on through another way, then he put his hand back on the door handle and turned it.

The door would not move.

He pushed hard. He rattled the handle. He jammed his shoulder against it.

The second match went out.

The stairs down from the tower were steep and winding. Franny went round and round and round, her legs aching with the repetition.

Towser snuggled happily in the rug Thomas had wrapped him in.

'Why are you doing that?' Franny asked.

'There will be a riot if anyone sees a Dragon Dog. It's going to be bad enough getting you to the Wyvern Hall.'

Franny put out a hand to steady herself on the spiral staircase.

'Do you climb up here every day?' she asked.

'You get used to it.'

'Huh.'

At least they were clean and well-swept, no cobwebs, or spiders, or beetles.

'Are you in charge here?'

'In charge of what?'

'The castle.'

'No.'

'What, then?'

'The wyverns.'

Franny stopped, glad of a rest. Thomas waited.

'I thought you said there weren't any wyverns.'

'There aren't.'

'Then how can you be in charge of them?'

'I'm in charge of the Wyvern Weavers.'

Franny gave up.

'Go on, then.' She had got her second wind.

The steps went round and round. Franny's head followed them. When they came at last to the door out of the tower she stumbled and fell and was lucky to be caught by a passing soldier.

'Hello,' he called, grabbing her as she slipped. 'What's this?'

'It's all right,' said Thomas. 'She's with me.'

A small crowd gathered to stare at Franny. She began to feel uncomfortable.

'Make way. Make way,' said Thomas.

People laughed.

'Wyvern Master. Make way for the Wyvern Master, and the Black Bairn,' called the soldier.

People laughed again.

'What's the matter?' asked Franny.

Thomas dragged her through the crowd.

Franny had never seen such a busy place. The tower room had been clean and neat, but the courtyard of the castle was the noisiest, dirtiest, smelliest place she had ever been in. It had all the worst mixture of things from a shopping mall and a very run-down farm. Traders stood at market stalls, shouting out prices. Pigs snuffled round, dogs darted past them, hens picked their way carefully through wet straw. Towser poked an interested nose out from the rug, but Thomas held him tight and covered him again. Franny felt her foot squelch in something and she didn't want to look down to see what it was, but the smell that followed her was enough to tell her. She stopped, scraped her foot on a stone and then rubbed it on a fairly clean patch of straw.

'What's happening?'

Thomas was holding the skirts of his long robe so that they didn't drag in the filth. 'Market day.'

'Can we look?'

'What about the Wyvern Weavers?'

'All right.'

Franny still had a good look at the market, as they had to push their way through the crowd.

One stallholder picked out two apples and tossed them over to Thomas. 'Here, Wyvern Master. Catch!'

Thomas fumbled the first, and Franny scooped it up. He grabbed the second.

'Thanks.'

More people laughed.

'Flying tonight?' shouted out a butcher.

Thomas blushed, put his head down and pushed through the crowd. The butcher laughed at him. 'I'll see pigs fly first,' he shouted.

Franny had to grab his robe to stop him getting lost in the crush.

They passed through the section where stalls sold fruit and meat and vegetables, into a part where the fragrance of bread and spiced cakes and pies delighted Franny's nose. Thomas stopped at a small stall.

'Hello, Thomas.'

Thomas smiled shyly at the girl in her apron.

'Who've you brought?'

'This is Franny,' said Thomas.

'Felicitas,' said the girl, holding out a floury hand.

Franny shook it. The girl's face was familiar, but Franny could not work out where she had seen her before.

'Two pies today, then?'

'Yes, please.'

Felicitas wrapped the pies in paper and gave them to Franny, still warm.

'Are you helping the Wyvern Weavers?' she asked.

Franny didn't know.

'We're going there now,' said Thomas.

'You've painted yourself beautifully,' said Felicitas.

Franny glowered. She had never had much

72

trouble from people because she was black, but she had had some.

Thomas was enthusiastic. 'It's the best ever, isn't it?' he said.

'Now look here,' said Franny.

Felicitas rubbed her finger on Franny's arm.

Franny pulled back. 'Stop that!'

Felicitas inspected her finger.

'It's not paint,' she said. 'It must be dye. How will you ever get it off?'

Franny could feel the pies crumbling as she squeezed them hard, trying to keep her temper.

Thomas rubbed his finger on her arm as well. Franny jerked it away. She was close to tears. Anger at the two, combined with disappointment that Thomas should taunt her so rudely, were equally mixed in her.

'Oh,' said Thomas.

'What is it?' asked Felicitas.

'Look, I'm sorry.' Thomas faced Franny. 'I didn't know.'

'What?' Franny said it as rudely as she could.

'You really are black, aren't you?'

'Of course I'm black!' she shouted.

People passing turned and looked. They laughed again. Thomas shushed her.

'Please,' he said. 'Please, don't shout.'

'What am I supposed to do?' she hissed.

Felicitas was rapidly covering her wares, taking down her sign, rubbing her floury hands on her apron, which she took off and folded carefully.

'This way,' said Thomas.

Franny was unwilling to go, but felt she couldn't just walk off on her own. For all his rudeness, Thomas was the only person she knew.

The bakers gave way to rows of cloth stalls. Bales of wool lay hugger-mugger in piles. Brightly coloured scarves, silks, satins, and cheapjack, shoddy and worsted; all materials for all pockets were on sale.

There were more stares, more laughs, as Thomas and Felicitas and Franny passed. And again and again, there was the cry 'Flying, tonight?'

At last the market ended, and Franny was led through a small gate on the other side of the castle courtyard.

'We'll be there in a minute,' said Thomas in a very friendly voice.

Franny scowled at him and made no answer.

They wove through stone cloisters and passageways, arched arcades and low-roofed alleys, narrow corridors and dim lobbies. Franny remembered the cathedrals and abbeys that Gerard had made her visit with him, insisting that she see something of the old England, memories to take back to New England. He could have had no idea that she would soon be scurrying like a rat through teeming courts, still in use.

They halted at a small door, almost hidden in an arch on one side of the low passage. Thomas drew a large, elaborate iron key from his robe, turned it in the lock and pushed the door open.

'In you go.'

'What is it?'

'The Wyvern Hall.'

Franny followed Felicitas. Thomas locked the door behind him. Franny looked round in wonder.

Now here was a cathedral. But round, not like the long cathedrals she knew. An immense space reared up above her. Long pillars reached for a high, arched roof. The branched arms of the stone supports flung themselves wide, as their fingers laced together in a firm grip, keeping the weight of the ceiling from crashing down. No seats, no pews or benches destroyed the clean openness of the building. A vast, empty floor lay ahead of Franny, uninterrupted, save for the broad feet of the pillars.

High windows slashed through the walls, filled with smoky glass, casting a strange blue light. They bore no pictures, no patterns.

Smaller chambers must have led off from this great one, because Franny could see doors and entrances, arched openings, hidden rooms.

There was no decoration, no furniture, save one thing. High overhead, wings spread, tail twisted in flight, was a great wyvern.

A robed figure, older than Thomas, stepped out

from one of the chambers. He flung back his hood, revealing a mane of black hair, and a bushy beard.

'Who's there?'

'Thomas.'

The man came towards them, saw Franny, stopped, scratched his head, continued.

He looked surprised when he came up to them. 'What's the Black Bairn for?' he asked. 'We're not flying today.'

Franny's rage finally exploded and burst out from her like fire from a dragon's mouth. 'Stop it! Stop it! I'm sick of you going on about me being black. What's the matter? What's going on? What's it all about?'

The man raised his eyebrows. 'She won't do,' he said. 'She's far too excitable.'

Thomas took the man's hand. 'Touch her, Weaver,' he said.

The man touched Franny's arm. She went stiff, feeling like an animal at market.

'Look,' said Thomas.

Weaver inspected his fingers.

He touched Franny again. This time he looked at her first. 'May I?' he asked. Franny nodded.

He looked again at his fingers. 'We'd better call the others.'

'Yes,' said Thomas. He looked at Franny. 'I'm sorry,' he said. 'I didn't realise. May I explain?'

'You'd better,' she said. 'And it better be good.'

Felicitas smiled, took her arm, and led Franny across the wide space and into a smaller chamber.

'I'll fetch the Wyvern Weavers,' said Thomas.

NINE

'Wyvern Tale,' called Weaver. His huge voice boomed the command and it came back to him from the stones.

The great chamber filled swiftly with men in long robes. Thomas directed them silently, though they seemed to know where to go. They formed a circle, and Franny tried to count them. Thirty? Certainly no more.

The big man, Weaver, walked around the outside of the circle, then he began to move in and out.

Felicitas walked to the centre and stood still.

Thomas put down Towser in his rug, then he cleared his throat and sang a single note, pure and clear. The men, guided by Thomas's note, began to hum softly, then, one of them started to chant a song, in a strange, ghostly melody, with words that Franny could not quite catch. They sounded like English most of the time, but then, sometimes, like German, perhaps, or maybe Dutch. Franny puzzled at it but could not quite catch the meaning.

From time to time others of the men joined in the words, in a sort of chorus, then they sang different words at the same time, but always with the low, musical humming of the others in the background.

Thomas Kych stood up straight, his arms by his sides, and began to chant above the gentle singing.

'Many years ago, time out of mind, when the wyverns flew at night, peace was everywhere, and the land was rich. In those days, the people of this land did not go to sea. They did not know about the great ships. Then, one day, as she was walking on a hillside with her dog, a girl heard the scrape of spades, the thud of pickaxes, the dragging of a great weight. She stood, amazed, and looked around, but there was no one to be seen.'

Towser's eyes peeped out from his rug.

'The noise of digging and of work grew louder, then with a sudden jolt, she was thrown to the ground as the hillside opened up beneath her.'

As Thomas said this, Felicitas fell, and the humming grew louder, menacing. Weaver stopped and raised his arms.

'From out of the hill poured men, armed with tools for digging. They seized the girl and her dog and took them prisoner. More men followed, armed this time with swords and spears and other weapons. They dragged a great ship behind them, with a dead king, lying in state in its prow.

'They overran the country, making waste the fields and towns, they stole our gold and silver, burned our homes.

'We fought. We tried to keep them out.'

Here the thirty men turned outwards and raised their arms in attitudes of war.

'They were too many for us.

'Only one thing stopped them from defeating us utterly. By day they were safe from wyverns, because they do not fly in the light. But at night, when the darkness came, they could not defend themselves. At first, many died here, by the might of the wyverns. But then, learning their danger, they came only in the daytime when the wyverns were not there.'

'Where were they?' asked Franny.

Thomas Kych frowned, ignored her question, and carried on.

'We set a guard round the entrance in the hillside. Day by day there were battles there, as the enemies forced their way through. But each night the Weavers called the wyverns.'

Franny looked at the Weavers. A solemn mime began, in which in turn each of the men fell, and then was replaced by another, so that each took his turn to be defeated, then rose again to replace his comrade. Franny tried to count them. About six, seven or eight at any time were lying in feigned death.

Thomas carried on chanting his song. 'They seemed to have no end to their men, but ours grew daily fewer. It was only a matter of time before all our soldiers were lost and the land would be overrun by the invaders. People were angry with the Wyvern Weavers. They said it should be possible to call the wyverns in the daytime. The Weavers protested, but the people were determined. The Weavers agreed.

'The next night they did not weave the wyverns, and none came. They were safe because their attackers had given up coming after nightfall. Then, just before dawn, the Weavers gathered at the entrance to the tunnel. They formed their circle and prepared themselves. The Kych started to sing. The Weavers made the Wyvern Pattern. At a safe distance, the people watched.

Nothing happened. The sun broke the surface of the horizon. The attackers began to appear in the mouth of the tunnel. They saw the Wyvern Weavers, heard the song, watched the pattern. The Weavers feared for their lives, but they carried on. An army streamed through the gap, brandishing their weapons. The people fell back, alarmed. The Wyvern Weavers faltered, hesitated, but gathered their courage and continued their song. The army, greater than ever, streamed through, like a Spring tide against the rocks, overwhelming them. The people fled, but the Weavers continued.

The army formed a great circle round the Weavers and jeered and mocked. They drowned the Weavers' song with their own songs, and they stumbled round the circle making fun of the Weavers.

The leaders of the army, their best men, pressed on to the gates of the city, urging the others to follow, to destroy our people at last and win the land. This was the greatest and best-armed force that had ever come through the gate. They were led by a small man, powerfully built, with a cruel face and a harsh, grating voice. His name was Parsell. He had been the first to break through that day the hillside was opened, and he had been the one who had dragged the girl through with his own hands and taken her prisoner. He was never near to the action when there was fighting, but he was always loudest in urging others on. The men obeyed him promptly, but they always kept a wary eye on him, as though afraid of their own general. He flung his troops at the gate and demanded our surrender. He promised that we would be safe if we would only give in to him and his men.

'How could we trust this sly creature when his own troops suspected him? We refused.

'In his haste to storm our town he had allowed the greater part of his army to lag behind and mock the Weavers. Now, he sent a messenger to them, to catch up.

'The sun had broken clear over the top of the fields, and the Weavers despaired of their hopeless task. The army unsheathed their swords, and advanced to make an end of them.'

Franny listened entranced to this incantation. She had fixed her eyes on Thomas's eager face as he sang. Now, her eye was caught by a slow movement overhead, and she turned to look up. The air was disturbed, but she could not discern what was moving. Towser made a low, whimpering noise. She reached out and touched him.

'The Weavers stopped. They turned outwards to face their enemies.'

The circle of men in the echoing chamber turned out, except for those who lay, in an attitude of death, on the paved floor. Felicitas walked away and stood at a distance.

'Making no resistance, they waited for their death.'

The movement overhead grew greater. Franny searched to see what it was in the high gloom.

Thomas chanted fiercely, 'A shriek broke the air, and, for the first time ever, the people looked up and saw the shape of a wyvern against a blue sky.'

Franny felt a breeze stroke her cheek.

'The Weavers turned their faces to the sky and rejoiced. The people of the town cheered. Parsell saw his army driven back through the gap in the hillside. Many were ripped by the talons of the wyverns. Many felt the dragons' fire. Many were struck senseless by their great wings.

'The wyverns circled and swooped. They clawed and ripped. They swept their wings behind them and dived through the gap in the hillside, pursuing the terrified army. Cheer after cheer rang out from the besieged town, still surrounded by Parsell and his advance guard.'

Franny looked up and saw the great metal wyvern flying above her on a silent pivot.

'Without the support of the others, Parsell now led only a small troop against the whole strength of the country, gathered for one last resistance against the invader. The order was given. The gates swung open and the people, armed with clubs and axes and staves surged out against Parsell and his men. Seeing their danger, they fled. Parsell's force, unused to the ground, were clumsy in their flight. The townsmen gained ground on them swiftly, and would have overtaken them and defeated them. Parsell's men stumbled and grew afraid. Then, just as they seemed to be caught, the ground shook. The townsmen stopped, looked around, and saw the wyverns swooping down, folding back their wings and chasing the fleeing army.

'The townsmen cheered at the victory of the wyverns in the daytime. They raised their weapons above their heads and waved them in triumph.

'But there was something wrong.'

The circle of Wyvern Weavers broke up. The huge man with the beard stepped forward, towards Felicitas. Still chanting, Thomas followed him.

'The wyverns had flown into the hillside, every one of them.

'Parsell seized his opportunity and escaped.

'In their moment of victory the townspeople realised what they had lost. By calling the wyverns in the daylight the Weavers had driven them away forever. So now, we only weave in the daylight. To try to bring them back.'

The air settled above Franny's head. The wyvern came to rest again, no longer a magical dragon in flight, but just a silent statue, suspended in the chamber.

'The Kych, and the Weaver went into the hillside, to follow the wyverns and bring them back.'

Franny watched Felicitas and Thomas and the huge man go through a small door and disappear.

She felt sick, with a sense of loss. And she started to cry.

Felicitas broke the corner from one of the pies and gave it to Franny. She nibbled it at first, still half-sobbing, then bit into it, then looked up for more. She started to feel better.

They sat, with Thomas and the Weaver, in a side doorway of the chamber, looking out over fields and hills, the sea out of sight.

Thomas and the Weaver shared the other pie. Towser had bits from both.

'It was just that when the wyverns went I felt so sad,' said Franny.

They waited.

'Just like when my mother left.'

There was a silence while they ate.

'It was like that for us,' said the Weaver.

'You were there?' asked Franny.

'No.'

'It was a long time ago,' said Felicitas.

'How long?'

'Time out of mind,' said Thomas.

'What does that mean?'

'It means,' said Weaver bitterly, 'so long ago that no one believes it any more.'

'I thought you were there,' said Franny. 'You were mentioned. The Kych. The Weaver.'

'There's always a Kych,' said Thomas. 'And there's always a Weaver.'

'People don't believe in wyverns any more,' said Felicitas. 'They think it's just a tale.'

'We keep the old ways alive,' said Weaver. 'But it's a struggle.'

'But this place is huge,' said Franny.

'It's from when people did believe in wyverns,' said Felicitas.

'Some still do,' said Thomas. 'Not just us.'

'Not many,' said Weaver.

'You do, though,' said Franny.

Weaver bit into his pie.

'It's been a long time,' said Thomas.

'Did they ever come back?'

'The wyverns?'

'Yes.'

'No.'

'What about the people? The ones who followed them in?'

'No. Not them, either.'

'So what happened?'

'There was a new Kych, a new Weaver. It's a family thing,' said Thomas.

'And the people built this place,' said Weaver. 'Over the spot where the hillside opened.'

'Just here?' said Franny. She felt her skin prickle.

'Yes.'

'They built a small one over the ship, at first. Then the bigger one,' said Thomas.

'The ship? Is it here?'

'Yes.'

'Can I see it?'

'Of course.'

'Then,' said Weaver, 'they copied the ship, and we became a seafaring nation. We remembered the wyverns in the shape of the ships and in their decorations. The ships have wings, and wyverns' heads. But they stopped believing in the wyverns. Some people even say the wyverns were made up in imitation of the ships, not the other way round.'

'But the Kyches believe,' said Thomas.

'And so do I,' said Felicitas.

'And the Wyvern Weavers,' said Thomas, with a look at Weaver.

'And Parsell,' said Felicitas.

'But that was ages ago,' said Franny. 'There can't still be a Parsell.'

'There's always a Parsell,' said Weaver, grimly. 'He took what men he had left and he moved them into the girl's house.'

'The one who disappeared?'

'Yes. He fortified it, built parts on, turned it into a castle.'

'A long time ago,' said Franny. 'He's gone now.'

'What?' asked Thomas. 'Of course he hasn't.

He watches all the time. His Spies are always in the city.'

'There's always a Parsell,' Weaver repeated. 'And he wants the wyverns.'

'Why?'

'Same reason as us.'

Franny was annoyed. 'I don't know what you're talking about.'

'Whoever controls the wyverns controls the land.'

'Why?'

'Because they're the wyverns. Parsell wants them. If he could get the wyverns we'd all be his slaves. We're poor enough already. We've been poor since the wyverns left.'

'He could go through the gates,' said Thomas. 'The story says that if the Kych calls the wyverns in the daylight all will be well again. But if they come in the dark, then Parsell will win.'

Weaver stretched out his hand. 'He wants to grip them,' he said. 'So that he can grip us.'

'Parcel's Grip,' said Franny, but she mumbled, and they did not hear her.

'Come and look at the ship.'

They went back into the wide chamber. Franny enjoyed the cool gloom after the heat of the outside. Weaver led them to a tiny door, the one he and Thomas and Felicitas had disappeared into at the end of the rite. It was so low even Franny had to lower her head to get through. Towser kept close to her and she could feel his soft fur against her leg.

The chamber was long and low and dim. Resting against one wall was a long ship, with mast and high prow, bulging sides and fixed oars. Franny touched it, gently, enjoying the grain of the wood beneath her fingers. They stood on a raised piece of floor that allowed them to see on to the deck.

'It's beautiful.'

'The first ship ever seen here,' said Thomas.

'What's that?' Franny pointed to a shape on the deck.

'The King,' said Weaver.

'What?'

'They brought the ship here with the body of a king in it,' said Felicitas.

'And that's him?'

'That's him.'

Franny thought of her paper, and the mysterious instructions. 'Can I see the key?' she asked.

'What key?' said Thomas.

'From the Sleeping King.'

'I don't know what you mean.'

Franny stepped forward. Her heart was pounding and she was dizzy. She reached out and touched the edge of the cloth covering the long figure on the deck of the ship.

'Stop that!' Weaver rapped out. 'No one touches the Sleeping King.'

Franny hesitated.

'Go on,' said Thomas, quietly.

Weaver hissed, but he did not speak to Franny again.

She lifted the cloth, her eyes half-closed, frightened of what she might see.

The figure was wrapped in more cloths, tightly, with tunic and helmet and gloves covering him. In his leather hand was a large key. Franny, her hand shaking, took it from him. It was warm and heavy.

She let the cloth fall back into place.

'What does he look like?' asked Thomas.

Franny shook her head. 'I hardly looked.'

Weaver stared at her.

'How did you know about the key?'

She felt her courage returning in the face of his anger. 'I am the Black Bairn,' she said. 'I knew.'

Weaver glared.

Franny sighed and stepped back. She put the key into her pocket, shivered and tried to make herself think again. Then she came forward again and put her hand back on the ship.

'And this is where the girl disappeared?' asked Franny.

'Yes,' said Felicitas.

Franny looked at her and recognised her. Her face was the same as that on the statue on the village green.

Felicitas seemed to understand that Franny knew something about her. 'She was my family,' she said quietly. 'I'd like to know where she went.'

Franny found she could not speak.

'And where the Kych and Weaver left to find her and bring back the wyverns,' said Thomas.

Franny walked away from the ship and looked around, her eyes growing used to the twilight.

'Where?' she asked.

'What?'

'Where did they go? Where's the door, the opening?'

'Lost. Long ago,' said Thomas.

'Some say it was never here,' said Weaver. 'That this boat was the King's boat and they buried him here to honour him, that the wyvern story came after the building, not before it.'

'And what do you think?' asked Franny.

'I'm a Wyvern Weaver, aren't I?'

She nodded. 'It should be here, somewhere,' she said, running her fingers round the stone wall, as though looking for something. 'There should be a way through.'

Thomas looked at Felicitas, with excitement. 'Go on,' he said to Franny.

'If it was here once, it should still be here now,' she said. She pressed ridges and decorative embellishments in the stone, as though they were buttons on a control panel, or handles in a door. Nothing moved.

'What are you doing?' asked Thomas.

'Looking for an opening.' She carried on her search, testing, pressing. The other three watched her, waiting.

Franny worked patiently, searching. Nothing opened. 'What are you looking at?' she said, feeling their eyes on her.

They made no answer.

'I can't do it while you're watching. Why don't you try?'

They waited.

Franny was about to wheel round on them and give up, when her hand found a strange, carved figure. 'What's this?'

'What do you think?' said Weaver.

It was in a corner, near to the stern of the ship, which overhung it, blocking off even the little light there was. 'A person,' said Franny. She pulled it, like a lever. It would not move. 'Help me to see.'

Weaver approached her. He opened a tinder box and struck a flint. A small flame huddled itself to his hand, then grew, spread and unfolded some light. He held it close to the figure. Franny gasped.

The stone had been carved into the shape of a girl, with wide eyes and close, curly hair. All around, the stone was grey, natural. Here, it was painted, deep black, with all the features naturally coloured, and she wore a green gown, long and full. Next to her was a small, sandy-coloured spaniel.

'The Black Bairn,' said Weaver. He looked at Franny, searchingly.

'What's it for?'

'You tell us,' said Thomas. 'You knew about the key.'

'What?'

'We don't know,' said Felicitas.

'Who put it here?'

'We don't know that either,' said Thomas.

'I want to go home,' said Franny. 'Where's Towser?'

He jumped up into her arms and they huddled together.

TEN

A squat, stumpy man, with bristly grey hair, sat uncomfortably on the grass, high on a hillside, looking out in the distance. His eyes were blank and empty, fixed on no point in particular. He was not looking for anything, just looking. His hands lay on his lap, half-clenched into fists.

To his left, the land fell away in a sheer cliff, and the waves thumped against the rocks far below. To his right, the land stretched on and on, uninterrupted by town or farm, or lake or house. Hill upon hill arose, and woody slopes and flower-dotted pastures and meadows, in an endless procession of greens and yellows and blues, with the tiny scrawl of the path of a river far in the distance. Behind him, clinging to the hill, like a lizard fixed to a wall in the summer heat, a grey stone castle brooded over the land. Its walls were curved. Neither round nor regular, it writhed away in a form that confused the eye. A stranger walking round it would find it difficult to calculate its shape. If the stranger could fly above it and look down, the design would be clear. A long oval shape, bounded by a high wall, was the courtyard. Another oval, smaller, formed the keep. Together they made a body and a head. Then, on two sides, other walls enclosed smaller buildings, kitchens, storerooms, barracks, armoury. Finally, two long walls stretched out from the opposite end of the courtyard from the keep. These ended in a point and enclosed another covered-in area. Together these buildings made a lizard shape on the hillside, or a dragon, perhaps, if the stranger believed in dragons. The only gate in the wall was just in front of the high keep, and was intricately carved, as a dragon's mouth.

The outer walls of the castle, to the seaward side, were weathered and beaten. Moss and lichen crawled across them, giving them a green, scaly skin.

This dragon castle faced the same way as the man, looking far into the distance, to see, just, the outline of the town, and the tall tower of the castle, where Franny had arrived.

The man's eye was caught by a small movement, far away. He blinked, looked around and seemed to recall where he was, then he flicked his fingers and two large dogs, like greyhounds, which had been running up and down the hill, came and sat next to him. Together they waited, and watched as a small shape grew nearer, bigger.

The view stretched for miles. It was early morning when the man's attention had been caught. He sat until the sun was overhead. Shortly afterwards a servant stood next to him with a plate of meat, some bread, cheese, and a flagon of beer. The man ate his meal, and watched as the shape approached.

The sun was behind the castle wall when the shape was near enough for the man to make out what he already knew, that it was a single figure, on horseback, sometimes galloping, sometimes trotting, never stopping to rest.

'Go on,' said the man, and the hounds shook themselves, raised their heads and ran down the slope, towards the mounted figure.

When he was half a mile away, the man stopped, dismounted, and led his horse the rest of the way. He stopped in front of the man, bowed, and waited.

'Well, Caton?' said the man, in a harsh, grating voice.

'Parsell,' said the rider.

'Yes?'

'The Black Bairn is here,' said the man.

Parsell's face looked at first as though he had been stabbed, then he breathed out, relaxed, nodded. 'Good,' he said. 'Did she have a Dragon Dog?'

'I didn't see one. She was in the market place.'

'Alone?'

'With the Kych.'

Parsell grimaced. He reached out a hand and cupped it, as though wanting the man to drop something into it.

'It's about time,' he said. 'Bring her here.'

'The Kych will try to keep her.'

'You can kill him, now,' said Parsell. 'If you want. We don't need him any more. Go on.'

The Spy looked at the scraps of left-overs on Parsell's plate, the lees in the flagon. He said nothing, bowed again, turned, walked away, mounted his horse at exactly the spot where he had dismounted, then rode back to the town.

The crowd in the market grew strangely silent as Franny, Weaver, Thomas and Felicitas passed through them. Franny noticed the people looking at her strangely, almost with fear. She clutched her bundle with Towser wrapped in the rug, keeping him hidden. The easy bustle of her first visit had gone, and the people fell aside for her, making a clear path through the stalls. From time to time someone jostled her. She tried to look inquiringly at them but they turned their faces away from her gaze.

She heard Weaver speak to Thomas. 'They know.'

'Yes,' said Thomas. 'The Spies have found us out.'

Felicitas heard too, and she took Franny's hand and hurried her along.

It was a relief to be at the foot of the winding stair, even though the climb ahead was long and steep and made Franny dizzy.

She had to stop, not even halfway up, and take her breath.

'Plenty of time,' said Thomas. 'Don't worry.'

'No need to go,' said Weaver, opening up the quarrel again. 'You can stay here and help us.'

Franny had made up her mind in the dark chamber with the long ship. She was going home. Straight away.

Weaver had argued. 'We need you,' he said. 'You're the Black Bairn. You can bring the wyverns back.'

'And the girl,' said Felicitas.

'And Thomas Kych,' said Thomas Kych.

'And the Weaver,' said Weaver.

'That was years ago,' said Franny. 'They're all dead. If they ever went.'

'We can keep her here,' said Weaver.

Franny glared at him.

'You can't!' she said.

Weaver did not bother to answer. He did not need to.

'No,' said Thomas. 'She must go home, if she wants to.' He looked at Franny. 'Please stay,' he said. 'Just for a while. Just to try to bring them back.'

'No. I must go.'

'Why?' asked Felicitas.

'I want my mother,' said Franny, amazed at what she was saying.

So they had set off, through the market crowd, back to the castle and the tall tower, back to the door into the small room.

Franny looked round and enjoyed what she saw, the desk, the sunlight through the slits on to the cool stone, the high ceiling with the circling wyverns. If she had not wanted so much to go home, to see Gerard again, to tell him how much she missed her mother, she could have wished to stay longer.

She put out her hand to Thomas. 'Thank you,' she said. 'I enjoyed meeting you.' Towser struggled to free himself, but Franny held him tight.

'You won't stay?' asked Thomas, shaking her hand.

'No. I loved your singing, though.'

Felicitas kissed Franny's cheek. 'Please come

back, one day,' she said. 'I hope you find your mother.'

'Thank you.'

Franny looked at Weaver, who glared back at her.

'Goodbye,' she said, taking the door handle in her hand.

'I'll see you again soon,' said Weaver.

'No you won't,' said Franny.

He grabbed her arm. 'Leave the Dragon Dog,' he said.

Towser licked her face. The sunlight caught the silver tag on his collar and it glinted. Weaver seized it.

'It's just his name,' said Franny.

'Towser,' he read.

'See?'

He turned it over. 'My master's name is . . .'

'What's that?' she demanded.

Weaver started again.

'My master's name,' he read, 'is Thomas Ketch.'

Thomas looked at the tag.

'You're right!' he shouted. 'It says so.'

'Ketch,' said Franny. 'Not Kych.' But her voice trembled.

'Same thing,' said Thomas. 'You know it is.'

Weaver looked at her with an unpleasant expression of triumph.

Thomas held out his arms.

'Here, Towser.'

Towser wriggled free from Franny and jumped to Thomas.

Franny let her hand fall from the door handle. 'If Towser's staying,' she said, 'so am I.'

'Good,' said Thomas, with genuine pleasure. Felicitas gave Franny's arm an affectionate squeeze. Weaver's face remained triumphant.

It was not difficult for the Spy to find out more about the Black Bairn. The whole town was talking about nothing else. He made his way to the first tavern, flicked a coin at the ostler to look after the horse, then wasted no time in getting himself a plate of meat, bread and turnips and a quart of beer. When he had taken the sharpest edge off his appetite he wiped his mouth with the sleeve of his jerkin, took a long pull of beer, sat back and listened to the talk around him. Some of it was excited.

'I saw her.'

'She was black as soot.'

'We laughed.'

'He bought her a pie.'

'I thought she was just, you know . . .'

'But Felicitas was with her.'

'Then, on the way back . . .'

'I brushed against her, on purpose. It was real. It didn't rub off.'

'The Weaver was with them.'

'They're locked in the Kych's Tower.'

Some of it was fearful.

'I don't know what it means.'

'The wyverns will fly now.'

'They're dangerous.'

'Should be left alone.'

'Not right to meddle.'

Some of it was contemptuous.

'Black dye. She'll be a month waiting for it to come off.'

'What difference does it make?'

'It's only a bairn.'

'There never were, there never will be wyverns.'

'All right. A bet. Fifty pieces of silver says you won't see a wyvern fly this year.'

Much laughter greeted the challenge, but no one was willing to bet.

The Spy, who had feared he might arouse suspicion by asking questions, sat back, and contentedly finished his meal and his drink, then took another pint of beer and listened. It was going to be easy to get her and take her to Parsell.

In the darkness Gerard counted his matches. Twelve. He struck another one and made the most of its light to explore the room again. Still no other exit. The match started to burn his fingers and he shook it out. He put his ear to the door and listened hard. From time to time there seemed to be muffled voices. He rattled the handle and called, 'Franny!'

ELEVEN

The next day the town was full of excitement.

Lookouts were posted to watch the skies for wyverns. Many scoffed and jeered, but sooner or later everyone cast a hopeful eye upwards, just in case.

The Wyvern Hall was crowded out with the hundreds of people who wanted to see the Weavers conjure up the wyverns. People remembered the old stories, they remembered that the

Weavers were supposed to be able to summon the wyverns, and so they demanded it. They wanted the land to be rich again, and free from Spies.

'We've seen the Black Bairn,' they said. 'Bring us a wyvern.'

The Weavers were helpless without Weaver and Thomas.

'We just follow instructions,' said one. 'You need the Kych, or the Weaver.'

'We'll wait,' they said. And they did. They sat around, eating picnics, gossiping and chattering, making a holiday.

The courtyard round the base of the Kych Tower was thronged with even more people.

'She's in there,' they said.

'They all are. We saw them go in.'

'Come out!'

'Come out.'

'Black Bairn!'

'Black Bairn!'

The chanting grew loud and faded, started up and died down, as people showed their impatience and lost interest by turns.

The Spy wandered through the crowd, distressed at the turn events had taken. It had seemed easy enough to smuggle the Black Bairn away when he returned. Now, with the whole town wanting to see her, it would be impossible. At least he knew where she was. But he shivered to think what Parsell would do to him if he failed to deliver her.

Children stood on the ramparts of the town and flew wyverns, broad-winged paper kites with flowing tails and red streamers rippling from their mouths as fire.

Most of the people did not believe that the wyverns would fly, but they all longed to see the Black Bairn. Those who had been close to her on her way through the market, when they thought she was painted, boasted that they had seen her and privately kicked themselves for not having realised she was real when they could have spoken to her.

Weaver looked down contemptuously from the tower room.

'Look at them,' he said. 'Just look. Most of them have never seen the Wyvern Weavers. Half of them don't even know the old tales. They couldn't tell you what it is they hope to see. And not one tenth of them believes that we could make the wyverns fly, even with the Black Bairn here.'

Franny sat silently.

'It's not her fault,' said Thomas.

'Did I say it was?' asked Weaver.

Franny was stung by the way they spoke about her as though she wasn't there. She stroked Towser and thought.

'What I don't understand,' she said, 'is why you just don't go through the door, up through the pond and have a look for yourself. You'll see there aren't any wyverns that side.'

Thomas went to the door, grabbed the handle and turned it. He pulled and he pushed, but the door wouldn't budge.

'It's always like that,' he said. 'It never opens.'

'It's easy,' said Franny.

'For you,' said Weaver. 'You say.'

'What do you mean?'

'You say you came in that way.'

'Thomas saw me.'

'We may make mistakes,' said Weaver. 'That door never opens.'

'You're the Black Bairn,' said Felicitas.

'Come with me,' said Franny. 'We'll look together.'

'We could,' said Thomas.

'Why not?' asked Felicitas.

Weaver looked through the window at the crowds.

'I suppose we're trapped in here,' he said. 'We could try.'

'Come on,' said Franny. She could have kicked herself for not thinking of it before. It was a way out, and she wouldn't have to leave Towser behind. Once they were through he could run home.

'It won't work,' said Weaver.

'Try,' said Thomas.

Franny picked up Towser.

'Don't let her go!' snapped Weaver. 'Stay with her.'

She glowered at him. 'I won't lie,' she said. 'Come on.'

She opened the door. It swung free easily.

Weaver looked at it in wonder.

'Come on.' Franny stepped in. Thomas darted in after her, then Felicitas, then Weaver. She shut the door.

'Now,' she said, 'when I open it, we're in the tunnel underneath the pond.' 'See.' And she opened the door again.

The tower room was still there. Franny gaped. She shut the door, closed her eyes, wished hard and opened it again.

They were still in the tower.

'It's you,' she said. 'All of you. You can't go through.'

They all stepped back into the tower. Franny's heart was pounding. She had never doubted that she could just step through whenever she wanted to, even if it meant leaving Towser.

'Please,' she said. 'Trust me. Let me try on my own, with Towser. I promise I'll come straight back.'

'No,' said Thomas. 'Not with my dog.'

To her surprise, Franny heard Weaver say, 'Let her go.'

Franny went back in and tried again. Again the door opened straight back into the tower.

Weaver smiled. 'Well?' he asked.

'No,' said Franny.

'Try without the dog,' he suggested.

Franny hesitated. She gave Towser to Thomas. 'I'll be straight back,' she promised. And, to her disappointment and fear, she was. 'I'm stuck,' she said. 'It doesn't go anywhere. I just come straight back. What's going on?'

'The gates are always like that,' said Thomas. 'Sometimes they open. Sometimes they don't.'

'But I've got to get home,' said Franny. 'I've got to. Gerard will be desperate. My dad.'

'What shall we do?' Thomas asked Weaver.

'We could go to the Wyvern Hall,' said Felicitas. 'And you could weave. That might work this time. With her here, and the Dragon Dog. They might come. And then the gate might open again.'

'No,' said Weaver.

'No!' said Franny, even louder and in a more determined voice. 'You broke the spell,' she said to Thomas. 'You stopped me going home. If you hadn't all come in the room it would have worked. I know it would.'

'No,' said Weaver, quietly. 'I don't think so.'

'What do you know?' snapped Franny.

Weaver looked down at her, his big figure threatening in the loose robe, his face half-hidden in his beard. 'Shall I tell you?' he asked.

'I don't want to know anything from you,' said Franny.

'I do,' said Felicitas.

'You?' He looked amused.

'I know I'm not a Weaver. I only stand in for the Black Bairn, and I'm not a Kych, but I believe in the wyverns. You don't.'

Weaver looked surprised.

'Of course he does,' said Thomas. 'He's the Weaver.'

'Only because he was born a Weaver. Only because it's all he's allowed to do,' said Felicitas. 'He doesn't believe in them. Ask him.'

'She's right,' said Franny. 'Look at him.'

Thomas laughed.

'Go on,' said Felicitas. 'Ask him.'

'I can't,' said Thomas. 'It would be an insult.'

'She's right,' said Weaver.

'No,' said Thomas.

'Yes. She's right.'

They all looked at Weaver. He turned to Franny, seemed to realise that he was too tall to talk to her, so he sat down, and began.

'It all happened, if it ever happened, so long ago. No one has ever seen a wyvern. When I was young I believed in the wyverns, I believed in the weaving. Every time we made the circle I believed that the wyverns would fly this time. Then I began to ask questions. Why was there no Black Bairn? It was foolish painting Felicitas black. She was still Felicitas. Why did we weave in the daytime? All the stories say that the

110

wyverns only flew at night, except for the day they disappeared. And why were the gates always closed? It seemed to me that the answers to all the questions were the same. Because it was all just a tale.'

'No,' said Thomas.

Weaver raised a big hand. 'Wait.' The sleeve of his robe fell away, revealing a snake tattooed on the forearm. He stared at Franny. 'You are black?' he said. 'Really?'

'Yes.'

'You always have been?'

She laughed. If anyone at home had asked her she would have fought them, but she knew this question wasn't the same as theirs. 'Yes. Always. You should see my dad.'

He nodded. 'How did you get here?'

'Through that door. It leads to a tunnel that comes up in the middle of a dried-out pond. I told you last night.'

Weaver stood up, stepped into the room, 'Not any more, though,' he said.

Franny suddenly realised what he meant. 'I came in through there,' she said, with a trace of anger in her voice. 'I'm not a liar.'

'No.'

'All right.'

Weaver sat down again.

'How could you do it?' asked Thomas.

'Eh?'

'How could you weave when you don't believe?'

'I'm a Weaver. I can do nothing else. I'm allowed to do nothing else. I'll tell you one thing, though,' he added.

'What's that?' asked Thomas.

'If she is the Black Bairn, and she came through that door . . .' He pointed.

'I did,' said Franny.

'And if this is a Dragon Dog . . .'

'Yes,' said Thomas.

'Then I think there are wyverns, and they will fly.'

Thomas breathed out slowly and smiled.

'And that means danger,' said Weaver. 'Great danger.'

'He's right,' said Felicitas.

'Why?' demanded Franny.

'From Parsell,' said Thomas.

Weaver nodded. A hollow boom shook through the room as a giant wave broke against the rocks far below.

'So we'll have to do something, and quick,' said Weaver.

'I want to go home,' said Franny.

'Then we'll have to weave,' said the big man. 'It's our only hope.' He sprang to his feet. 'A Black Bairn,' he said. 'And a Dragon Dog.' His eyes were bright. 'We'll weave wyverns.'

'And open the gate?' asked Franny.

'And open the gate,' promised Weaver. 'In

the daylight.'

Thomas took Franny's hand. 'You'll get your wish,' he said. 'When the wyverns fly.'

'Let's go,' said Franny.

'We can't,' said Felicitas.

'What?'

'She's right,' agreed Thomas.

'What's the matter?'

'It's Parsell's Spies. They'll stop us. We'll never get as far as the Wyvern Hall,' said Weaver.

'Why?'

'Because they need the wyverns for him,' said Thomas. 'I told you.'

'I still don't know why.'

'Neither do we, really,' said Weaver. 'It's just how it is. Either you're on our side, or you're on his. That's the way it is.'

'So what shall we do?'

'I know,' said Felicitas.

TWELVE

Caton managed to push his way to the front of the crowd. He could reach out his hand and touch the heavy wooden door to the tower. There was no other way out. All he had to do now was wait.

And the crowd was getting impatient.

The holiday atmosphere was turning unpleasant, and Caton was doing all he could to help to make people more angry and unpleasant.

A sly whisper here that the Black Bairn was too proud to show herself; a nasty hint there that the Kych wanted to charge them money to see her; an unpleasant suggestion there that the Weaver had kidnapped the Black Bairn and was going to use her to call up the wyverns and take power for himself: all of these were mentioned by Caton as he waited.

The crowd began to chant, more threateningly than hopefully.

Caton was looking round with satisfaction when there was a rattling from the inside of the door.

The crowd fell silent, then buzzed with anticipation.

The noise of bolts being drawn back, and a heavy key turning made them all attentive.

The door opened.

The crowd cheered.

Weaver stood in the doorway.

The cheering rose, louder and louder.

Weaver raised his arms and the crowd stopped, catching their breath.

'Stand back!' he called into the silence.

No one moved.

'We will not come through until you make a path for us,' he said.

'Black Bairn!' shouted Caton, trying to unsettle Weaver and steal his authority.

One or two others joined in. Weaver glared at

them, his huge face set behind the black beard. They faltered and then stopped. Silence again.

'Will you move?' he roared.

The crowd parted and a path appeared, snaking along through the market place and towards the Wyvern Hall.

'No one is to touch the Black Bairn,' said Weaver. He lowered his arm and stepped back. He re-emerged from the darkness of the doorway, with a small figure beside him, covered in a veil, her black face just visible beneath the cloth. She was dressed for the weaving. The crowd gasped and fell back, making the pathway wider still.

Weaver put his arm round her and led her through, towards the Wyvern Hall. Caton tried to follow but, as the two figures passed, the crowd surged round them, closing the gap. He elbowed and jostled his way through, cursing himself for allowing Weaver to take him off guard. He would never be able to capture her in this press of people.

The carnival spirit was coming back to the crowd. They were pleased that something was going to happen at last.

Caton shoved forward.

'Here, you,' said a big man, the butcher who had mocked Thomas in the market. 'Get back.'

'He was causing trouble,' said another.

'Get out.'

Caton was pushed and shoved, further and

further back, until Weaver and the veiled figure were out of his sight. He was kicked and trampled. He fell and had to squirm to get out of the way of wild feet, running to follow the Weaver. In his alarm he banged his elbow and a stab of pain shot up his arm, making his eyes wet. When his vision had cleared he was alone on the steps of the tower, the door open in front of him. The crowd had followed Weaver.

Rubbing his elbow he hoisted himself to his feet, and, with a curse, set off after them, no plan in his head, but a desperate fear that he must, somehow, get hold of the Black Bairn for Parsell. He had seen men who had failed to obey orders, and he knew that Parsell always caught up with them, always made them pay the price of failure. Once, not long ago, he had seen a man hung up by his ankles and lowered head first into a pit full of angry . . . but here he stopped remembering, shuddered, and looked around.

Parsell's Spies were in many places in the town. Few of them knew one another. It was safer that way – for Parsell. There might be a face even now looking down on him from a casement, or eyes following him from a darkened doorway. He had no doubt that Parsell had sent a message after him, to make sure he was watched, that his task was done. Parsell's grip was large, and it was tight.

He caught a small movement in a doorway,

and he darted into shadow. His eyes were flicking everywhere in panic.

The empty courtyard was an open trap.

He watched, breathless, as a small figure stepped out from the tower door. It was holding a book close to its chest. It looked round cautiously, nodded, went back in, then came out again, this time with another figure, the same height, robed to the ground, clutching a small bundle in a rug.

Caton recognised the Kych. But he was astonished to see the other figure, half-hidden in the long robe.

The bundle twitched. The figure gripped it tightly.

The bundle squirmed and gave a small yelp of discomfort.

'Shush, Towser!'

A sandy head stuck up out of the bundle and licked the figure's face.

Thomas Kych grabbed her arm.

'Hurry! We've got to get away, before anyone sees us.'

The bundle twisted round, and a small dog jumped out. It pranced around delightedly, freed from its restraint.

Caton, without a thought, put his fingers in his mouth, and whistled.

The shrill sound echoed round the courtyard.

The Kych jumped, nearly out of his grey robe.

The Black Bairn, for Caton could now see her

face as she flung off her hood to look round, grabbed at the dog. But it was too fast for her, and it bolted towards Caton.

Caton scooped it up, turned his back and ran.

'Stop!' yelled the Kych.

The Black Bairn shrieked.

Caton lowered his head and charged forward.

Thomas set off after him, tripped on his robe and fell. Franny tripped on Thomas and fell on top of him.

By the time they had got to their feet Caton was out of sight. The maze of alleys and yards had swallowed him up.

Franny tugged off the loose gown and sprinted round in her shorts and shirt, calling, 'Towser! Towser!'

The call rang out and came back to her, bounced from the ends of the lanes and the walls of the huddled houses. But no answering bark returned.

Thomas ran after her, getting tangled in the two robes, his own and Franny's, and always guarding his precious book. She was always well ahead of him, but he never lost track of her because of her loud calls to Towser.

By the time he caught up she was slumped against a wall, breathless, wet-faced and desolate.

'I'll never get home, now,' she sobbed. 'Never. I'm stuck here for ever.'

'Here,' said Thomas, helping her back on with her gown.

'Oh, Gerard,' she said. 'Where are you? Please. Come and help. Get me back.'

Thomas fastened the gown and Franny dragged its sleeve over her face and sobbed.

'I've got a plan,' said Thomas.

Gerard struck a fourth match and looked at his watch. Only five minutes. He thought it had been longer. He put his ear to the door. It was silent now. The match burned his fingers and he went back into the darkness.

THIRTEEN

The interested buzz in the Wyvern Hall dropped to a silence as Weaver and the robed figure entered. All eyes turned towards them.

The crowd that had followed from the court-yard squeezed to get in. Many were left outside. Even people who had hardly heard the old Wyvern Weaving stories seemed to know that they were not allowed into the central circle of the Hall, so Weaver had a clear, open space. He faced the silent audience and drew a deep breath.

'There are Parsell's Spies in here!' he boomed.

Silence.

'Look around you. Who do you know?'

The people looked, uncertainly.

'Come on. There will be no weaving . . .' He paused. There was a low murmur of disapproval. '. . . until Parsell's men are thrown out. Spies. Cheats. Thieves. They want to betray our town to Parsell. You know them. Throw them out.'

There was a small scuffle and a man was pushed forward and into the clear space. The Weavers rushed forward, grabbed him and thrust him back, out of the ring of stone pillars.

'More,' demanded Weaver.

The Weavers fastened the man to his pillar and waited.

A fight broke out near to the door. A man was pushing his way through, trying to get out. He was lifted over the heads of the crowd and bundled back like a sack.

The Weavers grabbed him and fastened him to another pillar.

Weaver whispered to the small robed figure, who kept close to him. They both looked to the rear of the hall.

More fights were bringing more men to the front. Each was seized eagerly by the Weavers and made fast.

There was a sense of relief in the crowd. No

one ever talked about Parsell or his men. Everyone knew about the Spies, but they were feared and hated, so they were ignored, or treated with polite courtesy.

This sudden ability to recognise them openly and to bundle them into captivity felt like the first morning after an illness.

The buzz and the laughter made the crowd relaxed and expectant. They looked up at the huge metal wyvern poised above them and they sighed.

The Weavers were running round the Hall, trying to keep up with the sudden and overwhelming number of men they had to fasten to the pillars.

Weaver stopped looking towards the other end of the chamber and started to make his way towards it. His face was creased with anxiety.

Now there were only two pillars without men chained to them by the iron hoops that were set in the stone.

'Count them!' shouted Weaver from the far end.

The Weavers moved, one by one, to stand by their captives.

'One!' the crowd roared, as the first one arrived.

'Two! Three!'

One by one, Weaver stood next to Spy.

'Fifteen! Sixteen!'

The counting rang round the stone Hall.

'Twenty-seven! Twenty-eight!'

Two Weavers stood, waiting.

'More!' called Weaver.

He was pacing about, tall and powerful, like a wild beast, hungry. His eyes were darting round.

'No more,' shouted the crowd.

'Two more,' Weaver demanded, pointing to the two empty pillars, the two waiting Weavers.

'Get on with it.'

'Weave!' shouted a voice.

The cry was taken up into a loud chant.

'Weave! Weave! Weave!'

Weaver strode forward and stood by the small figure in the long robe. He raised his arms, letting his sleeves fall back to reveal the snake on his forearm. The gesture silenced the crowd.

'Not until all the Spies are captured.'

There was a hesitant silence. People looked at their neighbours, trying to see if they might be traitors.

They waited.

One of the Spies sensed Weaver's nervousness. He banged his chain against the pillar, iron on stone striking out.

'Weave!' he shouted.

The silence grew thicker.

The iron clashed again against the stone.

'Weave!'

Another Spy joined in.

'Weave!'

Then another, and another.

'Weave! Weave!'

A wave of panic broke over the crowd and it shuddered.

The cruel faces of the Spies turned inward, to Weaver in the centre of the circle.

'Weave!'

The clanging and the chanting gripped the building in fear. The small figure moved closer to Weaver and its hood fell back as it looked up to him for help. The blackened, disguised face of Felicitas was clear to the crowd and to the Spies.

The Spies broke into a cruel, mocking laughter. The crowd gasped.

Weaver looked again to the rear of the Hall, with longing eyes.

The chanting stopped, as though by arrangement, and in the echoing silence the first Spy called out, 'She's gone! Parsell's got the Black Bairn.'

'He's a cheat!'

'Wait!' called Weaver.

'Cheat!' shouted the Spies.

'Get back!' warned Weaver, as the crowd began to move forward. 'Listen.'

Franny shook with sobs.

'Come on,' said Thomas.

'Where?'

'To get Towser.'

Franny gathered her robe round her.

'Weaver's expecting us,' she argued.

'He'll manage.'

'I've got to go home,' Franny wailed, ashamed of herself. 'I've got to find Gerard, and Elly.'

'You won't get home without Towser. He's the Dragon Dog.'

'So?'

'He'll get the wyverns. Weaver won't.'

'No?'

'No. But Towser will.' Thomas drew himself proudly to his full height, so he was nearly as tall as Franny. 'I will. I am the Kych.'

Franny sighed, wiped her nose on her sleeve, tried a grin, and nearly succeeded. 'All right. What do we do?'

'We go to find Parsell. That man was one of his Spies.'

Franny gulped.

'Come on.'

Thomas dragged her after him.

'Is it far?'

'Yes.'

'How do we go?'

'We walk.'

'Now?'

'When I've got some things ready from the tower.'

They were off again.

Parsell strode round his castle, stumping about on his short legs in a state of great excitement. He could not stand still, and nothing pleased him.

'I can smell it,' he said. And he sniffed the air.

Truth to tell, the castle stank, and the dark and dirty passageways he walked in his impatience were no place for anyone to sniff. But Parsell was not complaining about the stink. He did not notice the stink. He lifted his head, and drew in his breath and smiled a satisfied smile. 'They're on their way,' he said. 'I can smell them.'

And then he was off again, unable to keep still.

The dogs trotted behind him, long tails curled down, ears pricked. They sniffed when he sniffed, but they did not smell what he smelled.

He followed the narrow and twisting passageways. He went down into the greasy kitchens and scared the cooks. He ripped a sheep's carcass from an iron hook in the ceiling and flung it, whole, on to the roaring fire, where it scorched and sizzled and spat.

'Rotten!' he shouted. And he struck out and hit a kitchen lad, sending him flying, nearly into the fire after the sheep. 'Rotten, filthy meat. We need fresh.'

He found his way round the stone steps and the flagged floors into dusty, forgotten chambers, where spiders strung webs across the gaps in the walls, where the straw on the floor was rotten with age and infested with fleas and lice and rats.

He ran down again. Deeper this time to the cellars, and then through them to the dungeons. And he rattled the chains in the walls, and jangled great iron hooks and ordered his men to get them ready for a visitor.

He sprang, surprisingly nimble, back up to ground level, and crashed through a wide, long banqueting hall, not used for many years. Parsell's feasts were infrequent and fearful. He mostly ate alone now.

The dogs loped after him.

Parsell ran to the slit window and looked out. Nothing but the empty land. The dogs planted their paws up on the ledge, and their claws clicked on the stone.

Parsell sniffed, and smiled and spun round. 'They're on their way,' he said. And he was off again.

He ran down the stairs until he was dizzy with the spiral.

'Where's he off to, now?' asked a man.

'To the Grip,' said his companion.

The second man smirked, and the first man shuddered.

'Can't we ride?' asked Franny. 'I'm sweltering.'

'We'd be seen,' said Thomas. 'It's all open country on one side and the sea on the other. They'd capture us.'

Franny ran her sleeve over her forehead and brought it away damp. 'I'm getting out of this.' She tugged at her long robe and pulled it off, leaving it lying on the grass behind her.

Thomas stepped back and picked it up. He tied it into a bundle, with his book inside it, and slung it over his back.

Franny stretched her bare arms and raised them to the sun.

'That's better. You can leave that there.'

'You may need it.'

Franny shrugged. 'Suit yourself. I'm not carrying it.'

They trudged on, in silence.

Ahead of them, growing ever smaller, was the figure of Caton, and his horse. To Franny's eyes he looked near enough for them to sprint after him and catch him up.

'You'd never do it,' said Thomas. 'Even if he stopped. And he won't.'

'How long will it be?'

'For him? All day. Into the night.'

'For us?'

'Two days. Perhaps more.'

'It's hot.'

'And when we get near, we'll have to travel by night. In darkness.'

'And when we get there?' she asked. 'What then?'

Thomas smiled. 'Then I'll call up the wyverns. And they'll come this time. As long as we do it in the light we'll be all right.'

'Why?'

'Because I've got you.'

Franny nodded.

They trudged along again.

'But he's got Towser,' she said.

'Yes.'

'So, he can call them up as well.'

'Perhaps.'

'He can call them first.'

'Perhaps.'

Franny started to lose her temper. 'Then he'll beat us. He'll turn them against us.'

'He'll try,' said Thomas. 'And then it will be a battle. But I don't think he'll call them up.'

'Why not?'

'Because he needs you, not just Towser.' He squeezed his book.

'It's all in here,' he said. 'All the wyvern songs and stories, all the spells and potions. Gathered here many years ago. This is the Book of Thomas Kych.' His face was proud.

Franny heard the swish of their feet in the grass, the whirr of crickets, the distant crash of the waves. Her legs were whipped by the grass stems, and smeared with sap.

'I'm thirsty.'

Franny knew he had brought water from the tower.

'Later,' he said.

'I'm thirsty now.'

'The water won't last two days if we drink it now. There may not be a stream.'

'There might.'

Thomas walked on.

Franny thrust her hands sullenly into her pockets. She squealed and pulled out a paper bag and a bottle. She looked at the bottle, and turned it over and over in her hands. It was green, glass and not quite evenly shaped. The top was sealed with a cork. There was a writhing dragon embossed in the glass. It snaked its way right round the bottle, like a poison warning.

'Did you bring this?' she asked Thomas.

'No.'

'It's not the one I put in my pocket. It's different.'

Thomas smiled. 'I'm getting used to things being different,' he said. 'Aren't you?'

'I guess. But it's weird.' She put it carefully back in her pocket. It jangled against the key. 'Can I have some of your drink?'

'We must save it for when we need it. Drink yours.'

Franny took it out and looked at it again. 'I guess not,' she said. She popped a jelly baby into

131

her mouth and sucked it. 'Not bad,' she said. 'Better than I thought.'

Thomas frowned and walked on.

'You can have one if you like,' she said, when she finally believed that he wasn't going to ask.

'No.'

'Go on. I'm sorry I was mean.' She held out the bag.

Thomas took a red one. 'You're sure?'

''Course I am.'

'I mean, you're sure they're not real babies. Enchanted.'

Franny laughed.

'Do I look like I eat babies?'

Thomas hesitated, popped the sweet into his mouth and said, 'Yes.'

Franny laughed again. She looked at Thomas, stopped laughing, and shouted, 'You mean it.'

Thomas blushed.

'You do! You mean it.'

'I'm sorry.'

Franny was furious. 'You pig!'

'I really am sorry.'

'Why? Why do you think I'd eat babies?'

Thomas walked on.

'Go on. Tell me.'

'Well,' he said. 'Look at yourself.'

Franny was so angry that she walked faster and held her mouth tight shut. Thomas had to lift the hem of his robe and trot to keep up with her.

'You can't go this fast. Not in this heat.'

Franny ignored him.

He stumbled.

Franny pushed on, quickly.

Thomas limped after her, the pack on his shoulder dragging him one way, Franny's robe bundled round his book dragging him the other. He grew redder and redder and very wet-faced.

'Be reasonable,' he said. 'Does everyone look like you where you come from?'

This was too much for Franny. She stopped and whirled round. 'You mean black!'

'Yes. No.'

'Yes or no?'

Thomas panted and sagged in front of her. He was bent under the weight and the effort. Franny looked down at him.

'Both,' he said.

'Both?'

Thomas slid to the ground and dropped his burdens. He loosened the belt of his robe, pulled up the skirt and fanned himself with it, revealing very pale legs.

'I mean,' he said, 'you are absolutely the only black person I have ever seen.'

'Ha!' said Franny. 'You see. You . . .'

'Wait. Please.'

Franny waited.

'But you're also the only person who wears

such clothes. The only one with a Dragon Dog. The only missing person from the Wyvern Tale. The-the-the . . .' He looked around for help. 'The only person who talks about coffee and eats babies. What am I supposed to think?'

Franny flopped down beside him. She had tried to put herself in his place.

'You're right, I guess,' she said.

'Am I?' Thomas looked pleased.

'Yes.'

'Good.'

They trudged on, in a more companiable silence.

As the sun dipped down the air was filled with swifts, diving low over the tough grass and swooping near to Franny and Thomas, with no sign of fear.

Franny loved the wide circles they made and the sudden dives. She could not see the insects they were scooping into their beaks, but she heard the whirr of the scaly wings.

'Time to stop soon,' said Franny.

'Not yet.'

'I'm hungry.'

Thomas took a loaf from his bundle, tore a piece off and gave it to Franny with some cheese.

'While we walk?'

'Yes.'

'Are you eating?'

'Later.'

'My legs ache.'

'It will pass.'

Franny chewed, thoughtfully. This boy had never seen a car, a train. He rode a horse, sometimes. He may have sailed one of those long ships, but when he wanted to go somewhere, anywhere, no matter how far, he walked. And carried on walking until he was there. If it was a very long way then it took a very long time. He counted the distance in days, not in hours or minutes. He wasn't always looking at his watch. She had read about the old days, but never understood it. She began to see how strange she had looked to him, how unsettling.

'I'm sorry,' she said.

Thomas gave her a puzzled look.

'What's that?'

'I'm sorry I was cross with you.'

'That's all right.'

The swifts were just black shapes overhead now, against a dark sky, still blue, but only just.

'When are we stopping?'

'Before dawn.'

'Dawn!'

'It's summer,' said Thomas. 'The nights are short. It won't be long.'

Franny did a quick sum. Dark about ten, light about four? Six hours?

'I usually sleep at night.'

'Sleep when it's light. Then we'll walk a couple

135

of hours, then rest, then walk through the next night. By then we should be nearly there.'

'Arrive at dawn?'

Thomas bit his lip. 'That's the problem. We probably will. And that's no good. We need to sneak up, without being seen.'

'Then what?'

'We'll see,' said Thomas. He gave himself some bread and offered Franny some more. She shook her head.

'You don't know, do you?' she said.

Thomas chewed his bread.

'Oh, Gerard,' groaned Franny. 'Three days. I'm sorry.'

Far away, in the small stone chamber, Gerard heard a whisper and struck a match. Five gone. Seven to go. He tried the door again, but it would not budge.

FOURTEEN

Parsell's face was contorted with rage. Towser huddled against the wall and looked up at him with wide brown eyes.

They were deep below the castle. They stood on a narrow platform which stretched away on both sides in a curve. Beneath them, over a low wall, was a wide, round pit. The platform went all round the edge, like a gallery. Above them, a vaulted roof was almost invisible in the torchlight. There was no window, nor slit, nor opening to the sky. The darkness was all around them, in a tight grip.

Caton stood in front of Parsell. His face flickered in the contortions of the yellow lights from the flames.

'They tricked me,' he said. 'They tricked everyone. It wasn't my fault.'

Parsell glowered at him.

Caton wanted to be quiet. He wanted to run away. He wanted to hide. He knew that silence was best, but he seemed to have no more to lose, no more danger to face, so he babbled on.

'I brought the Dragon Dog,' he said. 'I got you that.'

'So you did,' Parsell's voice grated. 'So you did.'

'And the other Spies are taken prisoner. You said so.'

'All but one,' said Parsell. 'And he escaped to tell me.'

'But I got the dog.' Caton's voice was a whine of terror.

Parsell reached out a cruel hand and touched Caton's face. 'So you did. So you did.'

Caton shuddered at the touch.

'And you can use him,' said Parsell, 'to bring us a wyvern.'

'No!' shouted Caton. 'No!'

'Take him down,' said Parsell. 'And the dog.'

Caton struggled, and Towser twisted and

turned, but they were carried down from the gallery, and pushed roughly into the pit. Towser scampered about happily on the sandy floor, glad to be free and in the open again. Caton cowered by the door.

Apart from a stone building about the size of a shepherd's hut, standing against one wall, the pit was a perfect circle. In the very centre of the round arena was a tall wooden pole, like a ship's mast. Towser trotted over to it, sniffed, raised his leg and marked it for future reference. Then he looked around. All around the sides of the pit, set in the high, sheer stone wall, were doors. The one Caton crouched at had no handle, it could only open from the other side. The others had iron rings. Immediately opposite Caton was a door with a wyvern painted on it. Other doors had other paintings. One had a snake. Another had a fire. A third had a sword. Yet another had a gaping mouth, with sharp teeth. Caton's lips were moving as he tried to count the number of doors, but in the flickering torchlight he kept stumbling and going back to number one again.

Parsell laughed. 'Go on,' he mocked the Spy. 'Count if you can.'

'Let me out,' pleaded Caton.

'You can only get out of Parsell's Grip through the Wyvern Door. You know that.'

'Leave the lights burning.'

'You'll die when I open the door if the light

139

is burning,' warned Parsell. 'We can only weave wyverns in the dark in Parsell's Grip.'

'Let me try,' begged Caton.

Parsell growled like a dog. 'And waste you?' he snapped. 'No. We want to see how you do.'

'Wait, then.'

'What for?'

'So the dog can help me.'

Parsell hesitated.

'All right,' he agreed. 'Here.' He tossed a rope into the pit. 'You can mark the way.'

Caton tied one end of the rope to the embossed hinge of the entrance door. He held the other tight. The Spies in the gallery looked on, as Caton stalked Towser.

'Here, boy. Here.'

Towser looked at him, guardedly, then trotted over.

'Back to the door!' shouted Parsell.

Caton scooped up Towser into his arms and fled back to the door.

'Good,' said Parsell. 'Here's an offer. If you can find the Wyvern Door, in the dark, with the Dragon Dog, and mark the route with the rope, then I'll let you live.'

'Ready,' said Caton.

'Wait,' said Parsell.

Caton made a sudden rush into the circle.

'Lights!' screamed Parsell.

The Spies around the gallery plunged the torches into the ground and there was a thick, heavy darkness.

Caton kept running forward, and was struck in the shoulder by the post. He shouted in pain, fell to one side, tried to right himself, judged which way the Wyvern Door was and ran to it. He grabbed the ring, turned it, hesitated, and pushed the door open.

A scream of rage. Another scream of terror. A roar. A door slammed. Then silence.

'Light!' shouted Parsell.

The torches were relit.

The pit, all the doors closed, lay empty before them, save for the small, sandy figure of Towser, sitting right in front of the Wyvern Door, sniffing at it, and banging his tail on the ground.

'He found it,' said Parsell. 'In the dark. He found it. We can bring the wyverns through now.'

He threw a piece of meat into the pit. Towser ran across to it, and while he was away from the door the torches were put out again. When they were relit Towser was eating the meat, right in front of the Wyvern Door.

'Yes,' said Parsell. 'So we don't need the Black Bairn. All we need is the Dragon Dog and a piece of rope to hold him by.' His eyes gleamed red in the torchlight. 'We can go through the gate. After all these years. And get the wyverns.'

There was a disturbance along the gallery. A Spy approached.

'Yes?' rapped Parsell.

He heard the man's news and smiled.

'Good,' he said. 'We can have some sport before we go through the gate. Lock them up.'

'Those swifts are out late,' said Franny. 'It's almost dark.'

Her feet hurt, and her legs ached. Her throat was dry and she wanted a bath, but she did not want to give in again in front of Thomas, so she looked around for things to interest her.

'That's because they're bats,' said Thomas.

The black wings flapped over their heads.

'That's good,' said Franny.

'You like them?'

'We had them in the loft at home, in Massachusetts. I should have known. I wasn't thinking.'

'Take a rest,' said Thomas.

'No.'

Thomas stopped. 'I'm having a drink.'

Franny let him share the water with her. They made sure there was plenty left. She gave him another jelly baby and sucked one herself, to make it last as long as possible.

'Are you sure we're going in the right direction?' she asked.

'Yes.'

She looked up at the sky. She had never been so far from any city lights before, never seen such blackness lit with so many points of light. She had never worked out a constellation in her life and wished that she had paid more attention when they had been pointed out to her. It would be good to know whether this was the same sky as the one Gerard was looking at. She groaned at the thought of Gerard.

'Is it your feet?'

'No.'

'Do you want to tell me?'

'No. Is it the stars?'

'What?'

'Are you following the stars? To find the way? That's clever. Could you teach me?'

He laughed.

'What?' she asked.

'I could teach you about the stars. If you like. But it would take a long time. And you don't need them, not to find Parsell's castle.'

'Why not?'

'It's on the cliffs. Just follow the coast.'

Franny listened and heard the sea on the rocks.

'Let's go,' she said.

'If you're ready.'

FIFTEEN

'I thought it would be fun,' said Franny.

They were lying under the stars, munching the last of their bread and cheese. The night air was cool and Franny huddled in her robe for comfort.

'What?'

'Finding a dragon. A wyvern.'

Beside them a small stream interrupted the silence. Franny had held her aching feet in the cold water until they hurt, and then left them a

144

little longer until the hurt went and there was just a delicious numbness where the pain of two days' and a night's walking had made them sore.

Thomas had drunk until his eyes hurt. He had secretly been letting Franny have the small supply of water, pretending to drink when it was his turn.

'Not fun,' said Thomas.

'No.'

'The wyverns are power. They were the richness of this land, and now they've gone, we're poor. They were our safety, and now they've gone we're in danger.'

'Why?'

'Parsell's always there, always spying, always looking for a weakness. He'll find it one day and he'll strike. And there are no wyverns to stop him.'

'Why doesn't he? What stops him attacking?'

'He's never quite strong enough. Never quite enough men. That's why he spies and pries, pricks and hurts but never strikes. He'd lose.'

'Can't you go and beat him?'

'The castle's secure. And there aren't enough of us either. It's a balance. You can't tip it far enough either way.'

'But with the wyverns.'

'Yes,' said Thomas. 'With the wyverns we could drive him out.'

'Back through the gate?'

145

'Perhaps. Or at least far away.'

If there had been sunlight Franny would have been able to see Thomas blush.

'In the old days,' he said, 'the Kych was the most important person in the land. He brought the wyverns.'

'With the Weavers,' said Franny.

'Yes. So he was, well, important.'

'You're important,' said Franny.

'Not any more. I just sing old songs and tell old stories. No one believes them any more.'

'Parsell does.'

'Yes. Parsell does.'

'I wanted a dragon so that my wish could come true.'

'They don't bring wishes.'

'I know that now.'

'Sorry. I don't know that they don't bring wishes.'

The stream chattered on while they were silent.

'What happened to your mother, Thomas? You're all alone in that tower.'

'We'll have to go soon,' he said. 'And get up to the castle before it's light.'

'Mine went away,' said Franny. 'One day. I got up in the morning and she just wasn't there any more.'

'If we can get there under cover of darkness, we can find a way in. A drain, or a window, or a

146

gate left open. If they aren't expecting us there'll be a way unguarded.'

Franny sucked the neck of the strange bottle. 'So, I thought, if I could get a dragon, I could wish that she would come back.'

'I'm sure we'll find Towser, once we're in,' said Thomas.

'I'm sure Gerard wants her back as well,' said Franny.

'And then we'll call the wyverns – Kych and Black Bairn and Dragon Dog, we can't fail.'

'But now I need another wish,' said Franny. 'I need to wish that I can get home, to Gerard. He'll have the police and everything. He'll kill me.'

'They'll open Parsell's Gate,' said Thomas, 'when I call them. And you can wish and go home, and I can keep them here and call them every day.'

'Don't you ever wish?' said Franny. 'Don't you wish you were important, the way the Kych used to be?'

Thomas did not answer for a long time.

'She died,' he said. 'My mother died.'

'I wish she hadn't,' said Franny.

Thomas wriggled over to the stream, dipped down and washed his face. 'There are some things you can't wish,' he said.

And then he toppled forward into the water under the weight of the man who jumped on his back.

Franny sprang up and would have shouted, but a leather-gloved hand covered her mouth.

'No need for that,' said a voice.

Thomas was dragged, soaking, from the stream. His arms were pulled behind him and twisted until he shrieked.

'That sounds tight enough,' said another voice, and they were tied with thin rope.

Franny was shaking so much that he had to hold her hands still behind her back while he tied them.

'No need to go scratching round the castle walls like a rat looking for a grating. You can come in the front gate with us.'

The same darkness that Thomas had hoped would hide their approach to Parsell's castle had hidden the Spies as they came to capture them.

'Now,' said the biggest Spy. 'We can ride the rest of the way.'

'We'll all see wyverns tonight,' said his friend, slinging Thomas's bundle onto his saddle.

It was full dawn when they rode up to the castle gate and were swallowed by the dragon's mouth. A haze shimmered over the countryside behind them, and the day was preparing to grow hot and clear and bright. But inside the castle walls the air was damp and foul, and there was neither heat, nor brightness, nor hope, nor comfort. Franny huddled in her robe, clutching Thomas's book in the secrets of its folds.

Often, from a crowd a leader emerges. Leaders aren't always a good thing. When he led the hooded black figure through the market place and into the Wyvern Hall the leader was Weaver. When he demanded the arrest of the Spies it was still Weaver. When Franny and Thomas did not appear through the small rear door of the Hall Weaver clung to his authority. He explained, with some impatience at the stupidity of the crowd, why they had come a different way, secretly. He pointed to the Spies, chained to the pillars.

'What chance would they have had to get here with these snakes all around?' he demanded. 'They were to wait till all was clear and then follow. They should be here now.'

His tall figure, his fierce eyes and his clear voice held the crowd, for the time. They approved of the plan.

'They will come,' said Weaver. 'When it is safe.'

The Spies laughed in his face.

Felicitas took off her robe and wiped the greasy blacking from her face and hands. She turned herself back into a market girl who sold pies from a stall. It was easier that way. People stopped looking at her. But it also took her further away from Weaver. She no longer stood near to him for help, but she slipped into the crowd. She was not a Weaver, nor the real Black Bairn. Weaver noticed her go, but he said nothing.

149

The time went and no Kych appeared.

The Weavers stood by their prisoners and looked to Weaver for a lead. But others in the crowd began to turn their eyes away from him. They murmured, and they complained. They imagined plots and deceits. A few voices made more sense than others. They swayed the crowd. Then only two voices were heard. Then one. The butcher.

'Right,' it said to Weaver. 'This is what we want.'

The crowd held its breath and listened.

'You get us the Black Bairn. And you weave. We want the wyverns back.'

Weaver scoffed.

'You don't believe in wyverns,' he said.

The crowd hummed.

'I know you, Butcher,' said Weaver. 'When did you ever come to the weaving?'

The new leader hesitated. 'That's no matter,' he said. 'We've come now.'

The crowd made a small noise of support for Butcher.

'And you!' said Weaver, pointing. 'And you. And you. All of you, nearly. You know nothing of wyverns. You care nothing. Go home.'

He faced the crowd and ordered them out. For a moment he was winning. He had defeated Butcher. He and the Weavers looked safe from the crowd. Then, just before the first person backed down, a Spy clanged his iron chain against the pillar.

'Weave!' he shouted.

The crowd took up the cry. Butcher stepped forward.

'Out of the circle!' snapped Weaver.

Butcher stepped right inside.

'Make me,' he said.

The cry of 'Weave! Weave!' deafened their exchange of threats.

Butcher signalled them to stop.

'Now,' he said. 'I told you before. This is what we want.'

SIXTEEN

'This isn't true,' said Franny.

Thomas looked at her.

'There's no such thing as a dungeon,' she said.
'I know you read about them in books, but they're
not real. This isn't real.'

She looked around. The stones were slimy. The
floor was covered in stinking straw. Iron chains
hung from iron rings in the walls and from the
pillars. Rats poked pointed noses out of dark cor-

ners. Cobwebs trailed from low ceilings. Flaming torches burned with a smoky dim light that cast ghostly shadows on their faces. Thomas was chained to a wall by his ankles. Franny was chained to another wall, at an angle from him, also by her ankles. A guard in a leather jerkin rattled frightening-looking instruments. On the floor in front of them were two pewter plates with hard black bread on them, and two pewter tankards with rancid water.

Franny took it all in, for about the thirtieth time. 'This is a dungeon,' she said.

'Yes,' agreed Thomas.

The thick door opened, and a squat figure was outlined in its frame. It stepped forward and closed the door again.

Parsell came and stood in front of them.

'Thomas Kych,' he said.

'Who are you?' asked Thomas.

Parsell kicked him. Thomas curled up and breathed unsteadily.

'Hey!' shouted Franny.

Parsell turned and looked at her.

'Don't do that!' she said. 'Thomas, are you all . . .'

Franny didn't manage to finish her question because she was taken by surprise by the suddenness and the pain of Parsell's boot in her stomach. She decided to curl up like Thomas.

She heard the door open and close again, and

when she opened her eyes Parsell had gone.

Thomas was sitting up, looking very pale.

'This is not happening,' said Franny.

'It feels real to me,' said Thomas. 'Parsell's boot felt real enough.'

'How do you know?'

'What?'

'That that was Parsell. You asked him who he was.'

'I was being clever,' said Thomas. 'To annoy him.' He winced and rubbed his stomach. 'But not very clever,' he added.

'No, not very clever.'

'No.'

'But I guess it did annoy him,' said Franny.

'It looks like it.'

'Can we escape?'

'No.'

Franny was disappointed.

'We have to.'

'We have to,' agreed Thomas. 'But we can't.'

Franny leaned over and whispered. 'I've got your book.'

'What?'

'Hidden in my robe. I've got your book.'

'That might help,' said Thomas. Then he slumped back. 'No it wouldn't. Not here.'

'Why not?'

'This is Parsell's place. He controls everything that happens in here.'

'Can't we call the wyverns now, and beat him?'

'No, not even if we found Towser.'

'Towser,' said Franny. 'I'd forgotten all about him. Oh, I'm sorry, Towser.'

The straw near to her rustled and she drew away quickly, fearing a rat.

'Ugh,' she said, and she kicked out. Her foot landing in something squashy and alive. 'Ugh!' she said, even louder.

A small yelp was followed by a small sandy bundle of fur, and Towser ran out and flung himself at her, licking her face.

'Oh! Oh, you poor dog, locked in a dungeon.'

Towser grinned at her.

'He heard you,' said Franny. 'Now you can get the wyverns. We're all here. Come on. Call them up.'

'I can't,' said Thomas. 'Not in Parsell's place. Not in the dark. They'll come. But they'll ignore me and be in his power. He'll control them. And then it will be all over for everybody.'

'You don't know that,' said Franny. 'You've never tried. They might come and beat Parsell. Aren't they on your side?'

'They might,' said Thomas. 'But they wouldn't. Not while they were in here, in his power. If I called them up they'd destroy the land and he'd have won.'

'That's right,' said Parsell. He stood in the open door. 'Take them,' he said. Guards freed them from their chains and dragged them to their feet. A leather lead was slipped over Towser's neck.

'To the Grip,' said Parsell.

The battle was lost. Weaver was defeated. Butcher was in charge of the crowd and of the Wyvern Hall.

'We want the Black Bairn,' he said. 'Where is she?'

'With the Kych,' said Weaver. 'And the Dragon Dog.'

The Spies rattled their chains in derision. The crowd yelled their anger.

'See for yourself,' said Weaver.

'All right,' said Butcher. 'We will.'

And the crowd cheered.

The torches burned around the gallery. Franny looked up at them and shuddered. The smoke made her sneeze. Parsell split his mouth in a laugh. Franny pulled herself together, stood up straight and stared at him.

She looked magnificent in the flowing robe with her hood thrown back, her eyes bright in the torchlight, her hair braided and her shoulders straight. Parsell looked away, and Thomas noticed a glint of fear in the small man's eyes.

'We'll beat you, Parsell,' he said.

'I don't think so. Not now you've stopped hiding.'

'I wasn't hiding,' Thomas snapped.

'Locked up in your tower. Hiding.'

'That's my gate,' said Thomas. 'I don't hide. I guard it.'

'Coward,' Parsell taunted him.

'I guard it,' said Thomas. 'That's where the Black Bairn came through.'

'Thank you,' said Parsell, quietly. 'I wondered.'

Thomas hung his head, ashamed of his outburst, angry that he had given a secret away to Parsell.

'You see,' said the man. 'The gates are opening again. The Black Bairn came through yours, and now the wyverns will come through mine.' He kicked his foot in the sandy floor of the pit. 'And do you know how? The Dragon Dog will show me.'

'No,' said Thomas. 'He won't. He's my dog. He won't do it.'

'He'll have no choice,' said Parsell. 'But first, you'll die in my Grip. For here you stay until you try a gate. No food. No drink. Nothing.'

'We won't do it,' said Thomas.

'Come and see,' said Parsell. He took them across the pit. Towser stopped in the middle to sniff at his marker on the post and to renew it.

They reached the opposite side.

'This is the Wyvern Door,' said Parsell. 'Beware. If you open it in the light, then you die, instantly. Well, not quite instantly, but

157

interestingly.'

'But not if *I* open it in the light,' said Thomas. 'I am the Kych.'

Parsell nodded. 'You may be right,' he said 'But you won't be allowed to.'

Franny touched the painting. It looked and felt very old.

'If you open the other doors, either in the light or in the dark,' he said, 'then you meet wolves, or fire, or snakes, or . . .'

'We understand,' said Thomas.

'No one has ever found the door in the dark,' said Parsell. 'It seems that they always lose count. Isn't that remarkable? Guards, search them.'

Franny pulled back, angry. 'No you don't,' she said.

'We'll see,' said Parsell. 'Guards!'

A hand grabbed at her. Franny felt the book slip from its hiding place, and she kicked out. Her hand, which had been in her pocket, flew out, bringing a paper bag with it. It fell in the dust. Parsell picked it up. He opened it, carefully, looked inside. His face twisted in horror.

Franny took the bag from him, picked out a jelly baby and looked at it. She realised what he was thinking and she grinned at him. Then she bit its head off and swallowed it.

Parsell stepped back.

'Drag them to the gate!' he shouted.

Guards pulled Thomas and Franny back to the gate through which they had entered the pit. Towser snapped and growled at the men's legs. Parsell scooped him up, snapping and snarling, and carried him out. The door slammed and a lock bolt slid into place.

'Torches!' shouted Parsell.

The pit was plunged into darkness.

'We've still got the book,' whispered Franny.

'It's no use in the dark,' said Thomas.

SEVENTEEN

Weaver had no power to stop the crowd following Butcher.

'Don't,' he said. 'You'll lead them to danger.'

Butcher turned his back.

'Come on,' he shouted to the crowd. 'And bring them.' He pointed to the Spies. 'And the Weavers.'

The crowd seized the Weavers and the Spies, freeing the men from their chains.

'And Weaver,' said Butcher. 'Don't forget him.'

We'll need him.'

The crowd did as they were told, delighted that something was happening at last.

'What now?' asked Franny.

Thomas sighed. 'I don't know.'

'Can't you call the wyverns? You've got me and Towser.'

'Not in the dark,' said Thomas. 'They'll obey Parsell. I know they will.'

'You said that already.'

'That's because it's true.'

'What about just going through the gate?' asked Franny. 'Not calling the wyverns.'

'This one's locked.'

Franny tugged at the rope fastened to the hinge. 'At least we can find it again in the dark.'

'Yes. But no one's going to let us out.'

'They might.'

'Who?'

'Weaver.'

'Huh.'

'He might have followed us.'

'He's got enough trouble, I should think.'

'I guess,' agreed Franny. 'Will the people be angry?'

'Bound to be.'

'Let's try some other gates.'

Thomas grabbed her arm. 'We'll be killed. They're all traps.'

'We'll have to try the Wyvern Gate. It's our only hope. Let's have a look.'

'No.'

'We'll just listen. We won't open them.'

They held hands and set off, feeling their way round the wall.

Above them Parsell waited, his ears pricked. Towser wriggled in his arms, trying to get free. Parsell tightened his grip.

'You leave him alone, you bully,' shouted Franny.

Parsell snarled, more like a beast than a dog, and Towser went very quiet.

They came to the first gate. Franny felt round the edge, and underneath. A faint draught escaped, which brushed her fingers. She bent right down and sniffed.

'Ugh!' she said.

Thomas tried. The air was foul and stank of rotting meat.

The next was hot to the touch.

The next was shaky. Franny nearly pushed it open by mistake. She grabbed the iron ring to stop it and there was a violent thud against the other side, followed by frantic scratchings and a fierce snarling.

'Wolves,' whispered Thomas, 'I can smell them.'

They backed away and had to feel in the dark to find the wall again.

'Now we've lost count,' said Thomas.

'We already had,' said Franny. 'How many gates were there?'

'Thirty,' said Thomas.

'See,' she said. 'I counted twenty-eight.'

'Oh.'

'Let's go back.'

They found the hinge and the rope.

'Well,' said Thomas, 'do you want to starve to death, or get eaten by wolves?'

'Neither. There must be another way.'

'Let's think,' said Thomas. 'If we try to weave the wyverns, they'll kill us, in the dark.'

'Says you,' said Franny.

'Because it's true.' Thomas was very patient. 'But, we could try to open the wyvern door, go through and not call the wyverns. We'll be safe as long as we do that in the dark. We're beaten either way.'

'It's exactly in front of us,' said Franny.

'We'll lose our way in the dark, veer off, especially with that pole in the way. We can't even pace it out.'

'What?' shouted Franny.

'Well, if you stayed here, and I paced the circle, all the way round, we could halve the distance and that would be the number of paces to the wyvern door.'

'Yes!' Franny punched the air, invisible in the darkness.

'But we can't,' said Thomas. 'There's that stone

thing in the way. We can't go all the way around.'

'We don't need to,' said Franny. 'Here.' She gave Thomas the rope. 'Go to the centre. Find the post. Then pull the rope tight and walk back here the shortest way. Follow the rope back.'

'That won't help.'

'Do it,' said Franny.

Thomas set off.

'Are you there?' shouted Franny.

'Yes.'

'Make sure it's tight.'

'What are you doing?' shouted Parsell.

'Beating you,' shouted Franny. 'We're going to escape. And we'll bring the wyverns back. With torches, and light, and we'll get you.'

Parsell laughed.

Towser yelped.

'I'll get you for that,' said Franny.

Thomas stood by her.

'Twenty-five,' he said.

'You sure?'

He paced it again.

'Sure.'

'Good.'

There was a click, and a row of noughts blinked up at them from Franny's hand.

'Light,' said Thomas. 'Make it brighter.'

'I can't,' said Franny.

'What is it?'

Fanny sighed. 'Even if I understood I don't

think I could explain it to you,' she apologised. 'Trust me.'

'Is it magic?'

'I guess it is.'

She pushed buttons. 'Two times...' She screwed up her eyes and thought carefully, glad for once that Gerard had made jelly beans a reward for good calculating. She punched more figures. 'Three point one four seven, times twenty-five.' The calculator blinked the answer up to her. 'One five seven point three five,' said Franny. 'That's the distance all round. Now, halfway would be...' She divided by two. 'Seventy-eight point six, say seventy-nine.'

'Are you sure?'

'It's the best we can do.'

'Ready?'

'You pace it. It's your legs we're using.'

They set off.

'Are you going to try?' called out Parsell. 'Will it be the wolves? Or the poisonous smoke? Oh, I wish I knew.'

Franny pulled a face at him in the darkness.

'This is it,' said Thomas. 'There's no other door near.'

Franny swallowed. Her heart was racing. Was it three point, oh, who cared? It was too late now. She put her hand on the iron ring.

'Ready?' she said.

Thomas sniffed at the edge of the door.

165

'It's not good,' he warned.

Franny tried. 'Ugh, that's gross.'

'It isn't wolves, though,' said Thomas.

'Well, that's something.'

She turned the handle.

EIGHTEEN

Every horse in the town was saddled up and mounted. They rode full pelt into the night, and they rode hard. The moon guided them along the coast, with the crash of the breakers beneath them and the salt air in the horses' nostrils.

Butcher was at the head, with Weaver next to him.

'You're a fraud!' Butcher had shouted once.

'Not any more,' Weaver called back. 'Not now.'

'You've lost the Black Bairn for us.'

'Perhaps.'

The two men looked at each other with growing respect.

Behind them, streaming out of the gates, the whole town ran or walked, following as fast as they could.

Dawn broke, and the countryside opened in front of them; woods, valleys, rocks and plains, dells, sounds and wastes, and lakes, which when the early light broke on them, blazed like a wyvern flying round the sun. They reined in the horses, rested and watered them, then on to Parsell's castle, crouched distant on its hillside.

Parsell leaned over the gallery edge, his nostrils flared, sniffing for clues.

'What's going on?' he demanded.

His confidence that Franny and Thomas would open a door and meet a frightening, fatal enemy was slipping away.

'Kych!' he shouted. 'Are you there?'

Thomas laid a gentle hand on Franny's arm and put his finger to her lips. She nodded.

Towser squirmed and Parsell gripped him harder. Towser went tense and still.

Franny turned the iron ring and pulled the door.

It didn't move.

She pushed it.

Nothing.

Thomas tried with her.

It was locked.

'Is it the one?' asked Franny, in the quietest whisper.

'I counted,' whispered Thomas. 'And I think that all the other doors would open quickly enough. It must be the one.'

'We're stuck, then,' said Franny. 'You'll have to weave.'

It was lucky for Franny that she could not see the look of terror that flashed over Thomas's face. But she could hear the fear in his voice. 'I can't. I just can't. Not in the dark. It's not allowed. Not for a Kych. Don't you see?'

Their voices had grown louder.

'Oh, Kych,' Parsell mocked down at them. 'Try another door. Or weave, do. Let's see.'

Franny thought quickly, and she curled her tongue and whistled. Towser suddenly relaxed, and Parsell's grip on him was insecure The dog twirled free and leaped into the pit. He ran straight to Franny, hurled himself up at her and knocked her against the door. It boomed out with the impact and the iron ring clanged like the knocker at the door of doom.

'Try now,' said Thomas. 'Now we've got the Dragon Dog.'

Parsell roared out, 'Guards! Lights! Torches. Get them out!'

There was a flurry of activity. Flint struck against iron, and tinder nearly flared into light. But before the torches could be lit there was a scream, a shout of warning, a curse from Parsell, the noise of running feet, another, louder, stronger curse, and the gallery emptied.

Thomas grabbed Franny and prepared to fight, but no gate opened, no guard appeared, no torch was lit in the pit.

'Where are they?' asked Franny.

'I don't know, but we'll have to be quick, before they come. Try again.'

Still the door wouldn't move.

'You were wrong,' said Franny. 'You were all wrong. There's no door to the wyverns, no wyverns at all. You're a nobody. Your weaving is stupid. It's a joke. I'm stuck here for ever. And I'll never see Gerard again.'

Thomas was running his fingers over the door.

'There's a key hole,' he said. 'Hidden under the ring.'

'So what?'

'All we need is a key.'

'Huh.'

'I said a key.'

'Well, get one.'

Thomas waited for Franny to remember, but she didn't.

'You've got a key,' he said.

Franny felt so stupid that she began to argue.

'That's nothing to do with this. That was miles away.'

'Try.'

The key went in. It turned, silently, as though the lock was used every day. The door swung open. There was a brief gleam of light in the pit from the other side before Franny and Thomas slipped through, with Towser, and closed it behind them.

'Right,' said Thomas. His hand was shaking as he closed the door. 'Which way now?'

It was the suddenness of the attack which won the battle. The dragon gate gaped, unprotected when the riders arrived. They rode straight through its mouth and overwhelmed the sleeping guards in their quarters.

Butcher was not gentle in his treatment of them, and Weaver was hard pressed to stop him from killing them.

There was no plan, no discipline, no military organisation. The band of townspeople, startled at the filth and decay and cruelty of the castle, ran through it, setting torches to rotten straw on the floors and threadbare hangings on the walls. The castle was damp as well as decayed, and the fire made steam as well as smoke as it greedily ate its way through the rooms. It swallowed rotten timber ceilings and it gobbled up mildewed boarded floors in the upper chambers.

Weaver, realising the danger, tried to make them stop, but they ran on ahead of him in their delight at destroying their enemy's fastness.

'Find the Kych!' Weaver shouted. 'And the Black Bairn. You'll kill them all.'

Butcher ran with him, the two men united now in their plan to stop the burning before it was too late.

But fire is its own master, and once it is given authority over a place there is no stopping it. It raced ahead of them, and soon the place was a torch on the hillside, a beacon to the stragglers on foot from the town. The smoke reared up from its sides like dragon's wings.

And still no Parsell, no Kych, no Black Bairn.

Weaver covered his face with a skirt of his robe, soaked in water and he plunged down, ever deeper into the dark heart of the building.

The kitchen was safer than the rooms above. It was all stone, with no panelling or wooden floors. The high stone ceiling was already black with the smoke of ancient and countless fires.

Deeper and ever deeper, through the rancid dungeons, and at last to the tunnel which led to the pit, to Parsell's Grip.

Butcher kept up with him, step for step. The two big men stooped to make their way through the low passageways.

Spies had reached the pit before them, and Parsell was already waiting. He stood, protected by twenty men, in twos, facing Weaver and Butcher. There was no room for more in the narrow tunnel.

The smoke and heat curled round them, following them like a cat.

Weaver, once again in command, shouted over the heads of the men.

'Where are they?'

'Dead,' said Parsell.

Weaver stretched out his hand and pointed at Parsell. 'You had better be lying.'

'Kill them,' said Parsell, almost carelessly, to the guards.

It would be two against two, never better odds than that in the small space. The men hesitated. Weaver and Butcher were not armed, but they were big, and they looked dangerous.

'Go on!' he shouted. 'They're only two.'

Weaver stared at the two front men. 'Come on, then,' he said.

One lunged forward with a short sword. Weaver pulled the guard's wrist, overbalanced him, sent him flying. At the same time he wrenched the sword from the man's grasp. The guard made no attempt to stop himself falling. Instead, he hit the ground behind Butcher, rolled over and over until he was clear, then found his feet and ran off.

'Who's next?' said Weaver.

They hesitated.

'Will you let us go?' asked one.

'No,' said Butcher.

Weaver snapped out, 'Yes.'

They glared at each other.

Butcher looked at Parsell, 'Not him,' he said. 'The rest of you can, if you can get through the fire.'

The guards moved forward.

'Drop your swords first,' said Butcher.

'Kill them!' shouted Parsell. 'Or I'll see you all killed.'

The swords clanged against the wall and to the floor. In single file, slowly at first, then running for their lives, the guards pushed their way out.

Parsell turned, ran down a spiral stair and Weaver and Butcher were after him. They grabbed torches from the brackets in the walls and gave chase.

Parsell threw open a heavy door and ran through it. When his attackers found him he was in the middle of a wide, open pit, with doors all around and a post in the centre like a ship's mast. The door swung shut behind them.

Parsell snarled like a cornered animal. He looked round the pit, in search of something, but it was empty.

'Well!' he called. 'So I've got you. In my Grip.'

'We've got you,' said Weaver.

'You think so? Do you? Look behind you. Go

174

on. Try the door. See if you can get out.'

They looked round. The door had no handle.

'But there are doors,' said Parsell. 'Other ways out. Why don't you try one?'

'Where is the Kych?' called Weaver. 'And the Black Bairn?'

'Take a look,' Parsell invited them. 'Which door will you choose?'

The flames from the torches flickered wildly on his cruel face.

NINETEEN

It was hot in the tunnel, and the air stank, and there was a faint yellow light, flickering on the walls all around them that seemed to come from far away.

'Smoke,' said Thomas.

'From the torches,' said Franny.

'I don't think so.'

Towser kept close to Franny, rubbing against her legs.

'We have to go on,' she said.

'Yes.'

'Shall I lock us in?'

Thomas felt the door. 'There's no keyhole this side.'

Franny tucked the key in her pocket, where it clanked again against the bottle of poison.

'Doesn't your book tell you about this place?' she asked.

Thomas's voice was sad. 'It isn't as good a book as I thought,' he admitted. 'It's mainly songs and stories and recipes and diagrams. I don't recognise this at all.'

'Let's look.'

'Franny?'

'Yes.'

'Make a wish.'

'Why?'

'Because I want to make one as well.'

'What's your wish?'

'Lots. What about you?'

'Lots,' agreed Franny. 'You start.'

'I wish I could remember my mother. She died when I was very young. We couldn't make her well.'

'I wish Elly would come back,' said Franny.

'And I wish people respected the Kych again.'

'You can make them do that yourself,' said Franny.

'No.'

177

'I wish Gerard wouldn't be angry when I get back,' said Franny. 'I've been away about a week and he'll be mad. And,' she carried on, interrupting Thomas, 'I wish I was going to get back anyway, 'cause I still might not. And,' she hurried on, 'I wish he hadn't worried about me while I was away.'

Thomas waited till she was finished.

'I wish,' he said, 'that this tunnel was safe and went somewhere good.'

'I wish I had some jelly beans,' said Franny, pleased that the wishes were not quite so painful any more, and surprised that Thomas's wishes made her more sad than her own.

'I wish that . . .'

'I wish that . . .'

They had spoken together.

'Go on,' said Franny.

'No, you go on.'

'Try it together. See what happens.'

'I wish we could see the wyverns,' they said.

They giggled.

Then Thomas became serious. 'We'll always be poor and powerless and stupid until the wyverns come back,' he said.

Franny squeezed his hand. 'You'll bring them,' she said.

'I hope so.'

'It's a great responsibility,' she said, and she saw him not as a boy any more, but as an important person, who had a job to do.

'I must do it,' he said.

'If you,' began Franny. But she was interrupted.

There was a snuffling sound, and a scratching against the walls, and a noise, a bit like claws on stone slabs and a bit like rough leather being rubbed against the bark of a tree, and the smoke got darker and the flames flickered higher and the smell thickened. Something was moving towards them in the half-light.

Parsell's castle was a dragon of fire against the black sky. People tumbled out of it, through windows, doors, drains; some jumped from high walls and rolled down the hillside. Miles away, the townspeople who had followed on foot stood and watched its wings of flame fly up to the night. The advance party fell back from the walls, beaten by the great heat.

They cheered the destruction of their enemy and allowed the Spies who had survived to run off.

'All here,' said one.

'Except Weaver.'

'And Butcher.'

Felicitas, who had ridden with them, added quietly, 'And the Kych, and the Black Bairn.'

They became silent.

The pit was an oven, heated from all sides by the raging fire. Parsell moved away from the two men.

'If we're going to be cooked to death,' said Butcher, 'at least I'm going to kill you first. So I can die satisfied.'

'No,' said Weaver. 'Leave him alone.'

'This is nothing to do with you,' said Butcher. 'This is man's work, not Weavers'.' He stepped forward.

'No,' said Parsell. 'I'll show you a way out.'

'Go on then,' said Butcher.

Parsell ran to a door. 'Here,' he said. 'This is the safe one. You can escape under the castle and be free.'

'Show me.'

Parsell hesitated.

'I can't.'

'Why?'

'You need light. You need the torch. You go first.'

Butcher took the door handle.

'It's a trap,' Weaver warned him.

Butcher turned and gave him a superior glare. He turned the iron ring, then, at the last moment, seized Parsell, thrust the blazing torch into his hand, flung the door open and thrust him through it.

'Go on,' he said. 'You go to safety. I'll take my chance here.'

Parsell screamed as he hurtled forward. Butcher grabbed the door and swung it shut just as heavy bodies thumped against it, followed by clawing at the wood, snarls, yelps and growls. Parsell was silent now.

'Wolves,' said Weaver.

'Smelled like it,' said Butcher. 'We've seen the last of him.'

'And ourselves,' said Weaver.

'No way out?'

'Let's look.'

They examined the doors, stopping at last at the Wyvern Gate.

'This one,' said Weaver.

He tried the handle.

'Except it's locked.'

'It's coming to us,' said Franny.

Towser hid right under the robe.

Thomas was rigid with shock.

'Do something,' said Franny.

Smoke curled up from the wide nostrils. It opened its mouth and a small tongue of fire licked out then was gone.

Its claws, rounded like an eagle's, and thick and strong, clicked. Its wings were leather and brushed against the walls. Its tail was barbed. But the skin was covered with delicate scales which gleamed and shone in the uncertain light, colours that Franny had never seen before and that tempted her like jewels.

It was a terrible beauty and Franny was more afraid than she knew how to be.

The wyvern moved with a swift, elegant grace that surprised Franny. She knew now that it could leap forward in a second and be on them, savagely.

Thomas breathed deeply, let his shoulders relax.

The wyvern tensed, looked straight at Thomas, put its wings back and prepared to spring.

Thomas began to sing.

Franny could have wept. He was useless.

Thomas sang, not as he had chanted in the Wyvern Hall, but softly, sweetly, with a melody that enchanted Franny with its lightness and delicacy, but that made her remember days when Elly and Gerard were with her together, and she felt tears on her face.

The wyvern blinked. It put its head to one side, folded its wings, retracted its claws and leaned forward.

Voices shouted down from overhead.

'Who's there?'

'What's going on?'

'There can't be.'

'I heard.'

'Listen.'

Water sluiced down the walls.

'It's Parsell's men,' said Franny. 'They've got

us. They'll get the wyvern. Oh, Thomas, Stop. Let it go.'

Thomas's song faltered for a moment, then he carried on.

The wyvern backed away, into the tunnel, keeping its eyes always on Thomas.

The roof opened above them, just a small space, then more. Thomas backed into a corner. Franny looked up and saw a fireman's helmet. Then a fireman.

Thomas stopped singing.

'Anyone there?'

'Yes!' shouted Franny. 'Here!'

A flashlight shone round, finding Franny, but not Thomas.

'Just a minute.'

The face disappeared.

'We're safe,' said Franny. 'I'm home.'

'But I'm not,' said Thomas.

'You're safe here,' she said.

'No.'

'Please. Come with me.'

'I can't.'

'My wish came true. I'm home.'

'My wish was to stay. Remember?'

'But you'll die. Parsell will kill you.'

'Perhaps. But I called the wyvern. And it came.'

'Yes. You did.'

'And I tamed it.'

'No,' said Franny. 'I don't think so. But they've

come back to you.'

'No,' said Thomas. 'You're right. I didn't. And I don't think they have come back. Not yet. This is not your world, and it isn't mine. It's an in-between place. But I've seen one. I know they are here. And one day, I'll call them all.'

'Yes,' said Franny.

'And it knew me when I sang.'

Franny hugged him.

'What will you do?'

Thomas took hold of the door handle. 'Goodbye, Black Bairn.'

'Goodbye, Kych.'

He opened the door and stepped into the scorching pit.

'Here you are!'

A rope came through the roof. Franny grabbed it.

'Look, we can't make the hole any wider to send a man down. The roof would fall in. Can you hold tight?'

'Got it,' said Franny. She put Towser deep into the folds of her robe.

'Here goes.'

She felt herself lifted from the ground, and, just before she disappeared through the roof, took one backward glance and saw the leather edge of the wyvern's wing.

The heat the other side of the roof was like a punch in the face.

She was wrapped in a thick blanket. She was lifted from her feet. A plastic mask was clamped to her face and she breathed sweet air again.

Landed back on her feet she found herself owing her life to a man in what looked like a space suit. Faces peered at her. The wreck of the 'Green Dragon' blazed out the last of its life into the evening sky.

With a sob, the last standing wall dropped to the ground. Sparks flew up.

'What do you think you were doing down there in the cellar?'

'You were nearly dead.'

'I was disabling the gas pipe or we'd never have heard you.'

'It's gone,' said another voice.

'What?'

'The cellar roof.'

'Just in time.'

'Was there anyone else down there?'

Franny hesitated.

'No,' she said. 'I was alone.'

Towser poked his head out of her robe. Franny smiled. 'Except for my dog.'

'My dog,' someone corrected her. 'It tells you on his collar. My name's Thomas Ketch.'

It was a strange meeting. Thomas Kych, dressed in jeans and a shirt, Weaver, in a long black robe. And there was an old woman, who was Felicitas. She was so different Franny hardly

185

recognised her. Like Felicitas and yet not like. Like the statue, and yet not like. Hidden in years. Yet still the same person. The three of them stood and looked at her.

Towser ran to the boy.

'What's going on?' asked Franny.

'Here, look at this,' said a voice.

They turned.

The old pub sign had fallen to the floor, splitting apart. The green dragon had come loose from its nails, and when ripped away, revealed another, older sign, paint flaking, but still clear. THE BLACK BAIRN. A small girl, black faced, in a long robe, clutching a book, a key and a bottle, stared out at them. Underneath was written: KYCH'S REMEDY.

All faces turned to Franny, then back to the sign.

She felt her stomach knot, then remembered something.

'Where's Gerard?'

TWENTY

'Don't shut the door!' shouted Weaver.

But he was too late. Thomas let the gate close behind him.

'Open it,' said Butcher.

'You need the key,' said Thomas. 'And she's got it.'

The wall was hot enough to burn the flesh from your hand. The doors began to smoke. Thomas and Butcher and Weaver fell back, to the centre of the pit. Even there, the earth was growing hot.

'I'll never sell another roasting joint again,' promised Butcher.

'That's true,' agreed Weaver, grimly.

The doors burst into flames, surrounding them like a ring of suns. The air rushed in through the gaps in the walls, swooped up to the high roof, and, with a noise like a fast running river, sucked the flames high, lit the timbers and turned them into a bonfire.

'We're finished,' said Weaver.

But the flow of air upwards kept the heat from them. The timbers, instead of falling, were swept up into the sky, where they flew like blazing dragons, then were carried out by the wind, over the sea until they burned themselves out and fell, hissing into the waves.

In minutes, the intensity of the fire burned itself out, and the three figures were kept safe by the cool draughts sucked in from the sides of the pit.

At last, frightened, hot, sore and scorched, but not burned, they could look around at the thick stones which had been their protection.

'Whatever it was behind those doors, it's gone now,' said Weaver.

'Perhaps,' said Thomas.

It was all night and a day before the stones were cool enough for them to walk out through the open gateways, and the people, who had given them up for lost, cheered and greeted them.

Felicitas hugged Thomas and gave him some water.

'I saw one,' he said. He had not even told Weaver.

'Yes?'

'Yes.'

'Can you weave them now?'

'Perhaps. Soon. I think.'

They raced to Stone Pond. Franny felt sick with fear as she slipped into the opening. Weever and Thomas and the woman looked in amazement at the carved stone and the entrance.

Franny wrenched the door open.

'Gerard!'

'Don't shut it,' he said, and darted out.

'I'm sorry. I'm sorry.'

'Are you all right?'

'Are you?'

'Where were you?'

'In there.'

'No.'

They stood in the mud.

'Cover it,' said Weever. And he dragged the stone back into place.

A fork of lightning split the night sky.

'Summer rain,' said Thomas.

'Get to the edge.'

They sat under a tree, but they still got wet.

Runnels of water trickled into the pond. The mud deepened.

'It was just like I said,' said Franny. 'Just the same as this world, only different.'

'I was in there three hours,' said Gerard.

'I was there about six days,' said Franny.

And she told her story while the rain and the growing streams covered the centre of the pond and hid the stone.

At the end of the telling, the key, the book and the bottle lay on the ground in front of them.

'I guess these are yours,' she said to Thomas Ketch.

'I didn't get them,' he said, though he looked at them with longing.

Weever, too, looked greedily at them.

'You can have them,' she said. 'As long as you don't give them to him. They're for the Kych. And I guess that's you.'

'Thank you.'

'I need the book,' said Gerard. 'For my notes. I must have it.'

'No,' said Franny. 'It's his.'

'You can look at it. While you're here,' said Thomas.

'Make a photocopy?'

'No,' said Weever.

'Yes,' said Thomas.

'I guess that's the best there is,' said Gerard.

'At least we got through and no one was hurt,'

said Franny.

'Except Parcel,' said Weever.

'Hey?' asked Franny.

'Local man. He rushed into the Green Dragon like a mad thing, just before the roof fell in. We couldn't stop him.'

Franny was silent. Then, she said, 'Gerard.'

'Yes?'

'Can we go look for Elly?'

'I wish,' said Gerard.

'That's a start,' said Weever.

Mrs Ketch was propped up in bed, looking at the drenched ashes of the Green Dragon. Her face was tired with pain. Mr Ketch held her hand.

Thomas slipped in and sat on her bed. She smiled at him.

'I've brought you something,' he said.

'Thank you.'

Thomas drew the cork from the bottle and poured the liquid into a glass. It was clear, innocent looking.

He sniffed. A fragrance like the sweet smoke from grass rose up.

'What's that?' asked Mr Ketch.

'It's from Stone Pond. Thomas Kych's remedy.'

'Stone Pond's dry,' said Mr Ketch.

'Not now.'

'Let me try it,' he said.

Thomas pulled it away from him.

191

'It's for Mum.'

'You'll kill her with your concoctions.'

Mrs Ketch took the glass and said what they had never said to each other before, 'I'm dying anyway. They've tried everything. A drink won't hurt me.'

And she drained the glass.

'You're not dying,' said Mr Ketch.

'No,' said Thomas.